DEAD RECKONINGS

A Review of Horror and the Weird in the Arts
Edited by Alex Houstoun

No. 29 (Spring 2021)

DEAD RECKONINGS is published by Hippocampus Press, P.O. Box 641, New York, NY 10156 (www.hippocampuspress. com). Cover art by Jason C. Eckhardt. Cover design by Barbara Briggs Silbert. Hippocampus Press logo by Anastasia Damianakos. Orders and subscriptions should be sent to Hippocampus Press. Contact Alex Houstoun at deadreckoningsjournal@gmail.com for assignments or before submitting a publication for review.

ISSN 1935-6110 ISBN 978-1-61498-343-9

A Remembrance of Things Past

The joey Zone

STEPHEN JONES. *The Art of Pulp Horror*. Colchester, UK: Applause Books, 2020. 256 pp. $40.00 hc. ISBN: 9781540032973.

The artists of pulp horror could do it all.

The bodice-grabbing bony specter on the front boards of this book was originally painted by Norman Saunders for the comic book *Unknown World* #1 (1952). Saunders is now best remembered for the infamously gory *Mars Attacks!* (1962) bubblegum card series. At the same time Junior was playing with these, Dad was ogling Saunders's covers for "men's sweat" magazines such as *Man's Story*.

"Pulp" does not just refer to the popular early twentieth-century publications printed on coarse cheap paper that gradually yellowed, turned brittle, and acquired a sharp acrid smell, albeit one beloved by us collectors. Rather, it is a whole coarse aesthetic, somewhat yellowed in acceptability to some modern tastes, that perhaps always repulsed if not shocked its contemporaries. This volume, while initially seeming to lack focus, demonstrates this lineage of lowbrow, examining pulp through all media, from books to comics, from broadsides and posters to paintings and back again. Starting with *The Art of Horror* (2015), this third in a series of bumper art books by Stephen Jones might at first look to be table leavings of those previous but is instead a full meal in itself.

A strength of this collection is in its telling of this history from a UK perspective. Sarah Cleary starts by making the point that most editions of Gothic novels preceding the advent of the Penny Dreadful in the nineteenth century were too expensive and unattainable for the average punter, relegating shilling shockers to chapbook formats. This popular press was already slated for the cheap seats. Boys' weeklies such as the *Magnet* (1908–40) with Billy Bunter and his Greyfriars' chums appeared, as well as minor academies established by the likes of Edwy Searles Brooks featuring "Detective-turned-housemaster Nelson Lee, his assistant Nipper and the schoolboys of St. Frank's." More grown-up fare was offered in periodicals such as the *Passing Show* (1922–39) and *Hutchinson's Mystery-Story* (1923–27) as well as hardcover anthologies such as the Creeps Library Series (1932–37) edited by Charles Birkin.

Pulp stateside boasted artists such as Robert A. Graef, responsible for covers of the *Argosy* (the Frank Munsey publication starting in 1882) showcasing fantasies by A. Merritt and Ray Cummings. A new discovery for this reviewer was the superb linework of John Richard Flanagan, who started as a "stand-in" for that Australian mage Norman Lindsay. Flanagan went on to delineate the diabolisms of Fu Manchu, Wu Fang, Yen Sin, et al. As to that, there are six pages in this collection exhibiting that xenophobic trope known as "The Yellow Peril" inherent to the period.

There is an overflow of imagery that could have been in Jones's last book *The Art of Horror Movies* (2017). Paper ephemera is included from lost films such as the 1933 RKO version of *The Monkey's Paw* and, more famously, the 1926 Lon Chaney Sr. vehicle *London After Midnight*. An outstanding 2018 painting by Bob Eggleton channels Chaney's Man in the Beaver Hat, chromatically capturing that *face* in all its bug-eyed sawtooth slaver. Gregory William Mank contributes a foreword to the section on "Poverty Row" studios such as Monogram, which featured George Zucco, Glenn Strange, and recurring casts giving comfort in clichés of chills. As in the previous volumes, other contemporary artists offer tribute to these classic and not so classic horrors. Canadian illustrator Sara Deck designs a funereal poster for Val Lewton's 1943 film *The Seventh Victim*. *Rue Morgue* alumnus Graham Humphries is also amply represented with a 2018 and 2019 diptych(?) of the film 'set' Oakley Court, which has been used many times, from Hammer's *The Reptile* (1966) to Richard O' Brien's *Rocky Horror* (1975). Finally, there is the reproduction of a 1965 British quad poster for the American International Lovecraft adaptations of *Monster of Terror* (*Die, Monster Die!*) and *The Haunted Palace* as a double bill—oh, those lucky cinephiles!

"What ho, Chums—It's a Hodgsonian Horror!" From *The Art of Pulp Horror*.

Paperback cover art ranges from (the sadly recently deceased) Rowena Morrill's surreal *The Dunwich Horror* (Jove, 1978), complete with lizard skeleton yo-yo, to Hector Garrido's depiction of John Christopher's *The Little People* (Avon, 1965), which can best be described as Machen if adapted for a men's sweat magazine. Eric Stanton's 'sleaze' paperback covers clearly show the influences, if not the outright collaboration, of his studio mate, Steve Ditko. Toiling in these same pits of publishing, African American artist Bill Alexander is represented by covers for Myron Fass Eerie Publications' horror comic reprint magazines. His lurid funhouse styling mirrors that currently employed by California Bay Area painter Skinner. Other original 'comic' art by Lee Elias and Warren Kremer for the Harvey horror titles of the 1950s in some instances serve even more crispy grue beyond that of the legendary EC line.

Coda

On my fourth-grade schoolyard, I traded doubles of the 1966 Topps bubble gum card series for *Batman*. By comparison to the 'camp' TV show of the same time, there was more 'sweat' in the hairbreadth escapes of Gotham's Finest painted on these than under the makeup on Cesar Romero's moustache. Norman Saunders was again responsible. I can still taste those powdery pink brittle tablets that were enclosed in those card's wrappers. Proust can keep his madeleines—these will always remain my Communion Wafers to this lineage of Lo-Brow Kulture.

Stories with Soul

Géza A. G. Reilly

DARRELL SCHWEITZER. *The Mysteries of the Faceless King*. Hornsea, UK: PS Publishing, 2020. 350 pp. £25.00 hc. ISBN 9781786364425.
DARRELL SCHWEITZER. *The Last Heretic*. Hornsea, UK: PS Publishing, 2020. 387 pp. £25.00 hc. ISBN 9781786364449.

After finishing *The Mysteries of the Faceless King,* I started to think that Darrell Schweitzer has *soul*. By the time I finished *The Last Heretic,* I was convinced of it. With some reflection, however, I realized that I didn't know Schweitzer's religious beliefs at all—if he has any—so perhaps it would be better to say that these *stories* have soul.

I was struck by how so many of the stories in PS Publishing's recent two-volume release of Schweitzer's work deal with tender themes and do so gently. Many of these stories positively bleed yearnings for peace, comfort, community, and love—always, always love. Often, when those aspects of life are attained, it is in an unexpected fashion. Sometimes those questing after them (consciously or not) are violently or tragically denied them. But those aspects are always part of the warp and woof of the world in Schweitzer's stories. They exist, like the purity of purpose that the knight protagonist of "Bitter Chivalry" seeks after, and thus they remain things to be quested for even if their attainment is impossible.

This tender, soulful quality of Schweitzer's work is perhaps belied slightly by the story notes that Schweitzer has appended to both volumes. In these notes, Schweitzer takes the reader through a brief discussion of each story, why it was written, and what was involved in the writing. Often, Schweitzer's notes portray him as a man of wit and charm, divorced from the emotional tenor of the stories he discusses, and that could potentially tinge one's memories of what has just been read.

However, I think that Schweitzer might just be playing a magician's trick with his notes. After all, what better way to cover and protect a core of tenderness than to portray it as growing out of dispassionate soil?

None of this is to say that *The Best of Darrell Schweitzer* is a maudlin or melodramatic affair overall. No—while some stories, like "The Spirit of the Back Stairs," seem more like loving wounds than stories, others are pure horror, some are hysterically funny, and some are pure intellectual delight. "The Eater of Hours" is perhaps one of the most terrifying stories I've ever read, for example, while "The Last Heretic" gave me enough food for thought to last me for several weeks. And who could deny the effectiveness of the dark comedy in "Pennies from Hell" or "Kvetchula"?

All these strains of narrative pleasure are bound up in a wide array of genres. Schweitzer, judging from these collections, is at home in many places, but he has a particular passion for the fantasy genre. Many, if not all, of his long-standing fantasy worlds are represented here. Aside these are Schweitzer's historical fictions (usually involving antiquity), his Arthurian stories, his Lovecraftian stories, and even the odd science fiction tale. What is striking about this array is that Schweitzer seems perfectly comfortable with the genres he has chosen. Perhaps that should not be surprising in a 'best of' collection, but still, I think the adept way that Schweitzer moves between distinct genres speaks to the man's talent in general.

I was surprised by how many of the stories in both volumes, no matter their genre, focus on children. Often, these stories dovetail into a shared exploration of the loss of innocence or the denial of potential. "The Story of the Brown Man" in *The Mysteries of the Faceless King* introduces this idea in a quasi-historical setting, for example, while "Savages" goes into a contemporary horror scenario, and "The Mysteries of the Faceless King," "The Outside Man," and "He Speaks Through Those Who Do Not Die," while not being centered exclusively on children, do hinge on trauma incurred during childhood. While this repeated touching on childhood might result in a sappy, 'children are precious angels' motif in a lesser author's work, Schweitzer manages to present childhood—or more correctly *innocence*—as precious, but also a site of potential danger. More, I think, should be written on how Schweitzer approaches childhood and children in his oeuvre.

Of course, no collection is without flaws, and Schweitzer's two volumes do have some of their own. At least two of the aforementioned child-focused stories, "Savages" and "The Dead Kid," share the same location and general overall thrust, making them too similar for the reader to enjoy them fully in the same collection. Many of these stories, in fact, share a distinctly similar narrative structure, with narrators (who are only named in an offhand way deep into the story) discussing a person they met earlier in life (usually in college) and diving into backstory immediately (occasionally interspersed with tantalizing glimpses of the weird or terrible events going on in the present day) before moving on to how the narrators are reunited with their awful companion and what has led to the inevitable conclusion. This shared structure does not make these stories *bad,* by any means, but being able to see their bones by dint of them being presented close together does reduce their narrative power a bit.

The same could be said for how the stories are grouped together overall. The first seven stories in the first volume, for example, are all high fantasy or historical fantasy, which I found makes the eyes glaze over a little—especially if the reader is not conversant with Schweitzer's various fantasy worlds. Volume two manages to avoid this over-repetition of genre, which is to be desired, but there the stories seem to be paradoxically scattershot in their presentation. I realize that this is a completely subjective experience of the text, and other readers may not find the smoothness in volume one or the jarring movements in volume two a problem, but it did strike me as notable.

These are minor complaints at best, however. What Schweitzer has given us in these two volumes is a feast, and if some of the courses end up tasting a little bit alike, or if there is a dizzying multiplicity of flavors on offer, that does not mean the chef is to be denigrated. Equally, if a comparison of some dishes at the feast allows us to see the tricks the chef pulled in their preparation, that does not mean that the tricks themselves are badly used. Any 'best of' collection of Schweitzer's work is going to leave the reader feeling as though there is much more to the man and his writing than has been shown; these stories have soul, as I said, and whether that soul originates in the page or in the author himself, it is a soul that wants to be heard. We should listen closely.

A Few Drops of Claret

Daniel Pietersen

EDDIE FALVEY, JOE HICKINBOTTOM, and JONATHAN WROOT, ed. *New Blood: Critical Approaches to Contemporary Horror*. Cardiff: University of Wales Press, 2021. 288 pp. $60.00 tpb. ISBN: 9781786836342.

One of the things I like most about horror is its range. Horror can be represented across the full spectrum of media and found lurking within even apparently conflicting genres. I look back over the past few years and think beyond the obvious horror-homes of film and TV to examples like Tom Wright's harrowing stage adaptation of *Picnic at Hanging Rock,* the haunting and hauntological sci-fi horror art books of Simon Stålenhag or even Cryo Chamber's ever-expanding discography of sinister, abyssal dark ambient. Horror doesn't have to be, as Lovecraft famously asserted, just "secret murder, bloody bones, or a sheeted form clanking chains." In fact, horror is sometimes most effective when it manifests itself quietly, in an unexpected place. The word "apparition," after all, is related to the Latin *apparere:* "to appear silently, as a servant appears."

Which means that, to me at least, *New Blood*'s focus on film and TV horror—and often fairly extreme, gory examples of film and TV horror—feels, ironically for a medium that privileges the power of sight, slightly myopic.

That said, it isn't fair to look at *New Blood* based on what I would like it to be rather than what it is. Equally, in its defense, all three of the book's editors are involved in the discipline of Film Studies, so perhaps it is my expectations that are at fault rather than theirs. So let's dive in and try to remember that the subtitle of Critical Approaches to Contemporary Horror should really be read as Critical Approaches to Contemporary TV and Film Horror.

New Blood's essays interrogate a number of subjects; from

the history of horror film festivals like Cine-Excess, through the curiously resilient presence of Nazism (and Nazi zombies) in horror, to a discussion of sometimes problematic terms such as "prestige" or "elevated" when attempting to bring horror to a state more accepted by cultural gatekeepers. Out of these, however, I was fascinated by Thomas Joseph Watson's "The Kids Are Alt-Right," where he uses Jeremy Saulnier's 2015 film *Green Room* as a lens to investigate contemporary politics and political violence in the US (and, by extension, in the rest of the world).

Watson excels in not simply describing his chosen text's themes—something that a few of the book's other essays suffer from—but by engaging with how it both predicts and reflects the real-life horror of bigotry, fascism, and white supremacy while simultaneously revealing it as a standpoint based on instilling fear in others to hide one's own fears. Watson points out that *Green Room*'s villain Darcy doesn't necessarily believe fascist ideology to the degree he expects of his followers, but rather is "only really interested in protecting his own livelihood as a dealer of heroin." To do this, Darcy enacts violence against any threats through his underlings: he becomes "an invisible orchestrator of violence," initiating violence while hiding himself from the consequences of that violence. This echoes the claim of French philosopher Michel Foucault that "power's success is proportional to an ability to hide its own mechanisms," and Watson uses this to equate *Green Room*'s examination of specific violence to "a wider systemic discourse of oppression and control." Similarly, it is when Darcy is fully revealed near the end of the film that his power, and therefore his ability to instill fear, is diminished to a point where it no longer exists: "You were so scary at night," admits protagonist Pat. Although some viewers may think this is anticlimactic, I find it to be a very interesting, and strangely hopeful, inversion of the traditional horror film reveal of the monster in all its terrifying glory. Watson's great insight here is that horror like *Green Room* shows us that monsters can be defeated by showing us *how* monsters can be defeated.

The other surprise success in *New Blood*—a surprise for me, at least—was Neil Jackson's reappraisal of notorious "Euro-snuff" *A Serbian Film* (2010). Jackson positions the film as one that "defines sexual violence as culturally embedded" while, sensibly, not being over-enthusiastic in praising its qualities; he readily admits that the film is "doubtlessly crude, abrasive and hysterical." From this standpoint Jackson examines *A Serbian Film* as an attempt to work through the wounds of the Balkan conflict and its lingering trauma before widening his view to a broader investigation of "porno-capitalism." This is an interesting concept, as it implies that not only do consumers sell themselves to capitalism by buying its products, but capitalism sells itself to consumers by offering those products. This creates two options for those within the capitalist system: either continue within the increasingly extreme cycle of offer/purchase or attempt to resist it.

As evidenced by the events of *A Serbian Film,* these choices lead either to dehumanization or destruction. Like Watson's view of *Green Room,* the monster of *A Serbian Film* is, for Jackson, not the people who act out the film's narrative but the systems that allow, even force, that narrative to exist. I found this a powerful reading of a film that, I have to admit, I had initially dismissed out of hand. Jackson's argument that *A Serbian Film* goes "far beyond its manifest ability to run the somewhat limited gamut of shock, disgust and revulsion" is a compelling one.

Had *New Blood* included more essays of this caliber and had it broadened its remit beyond a Western view of visual horror—even the chapters on J-Horror are concerned with how Western audiences misunderstand the breadth of Takashi Miike's work to pigeonhole him as a horror auteur or how consumption of Japanese "Otherness" is often fetishized by Western marketing—then it would be an invaluable reference for the first decades of twenty-first-century horror. Even a more accurate description of the book's focus on that remit, which is a perfectly valid one, would have removed much of my frustration with it. Perhaps these frustrations are just a result of my being hypercritical, and I admit that it is impossible for one book to cover every facet of a genre as wide-reaching as horror; but *New Blood*'s presentation, as well as the Horror

Studies series' statement that it is "dedicated to the study of the genre in its various manifestations—from fiction to cinema and television, magazines to comics, and extending to other forms of narrative texts such as video games and music," doesn't make me feel that guilty about it.

New Blood is definitely a valuable text, especially for those interested in the more extreme end of the visual horror spectrum, and it is no doubt one I will return to, but I would dearly love to see a future collection that truly covers "contemporary horror" in its full plumage.

The Isle Is Full of Noises

Edward Guimont

KEVIN MCMANUS and MATTHEW MCMANUS, dir. *The Block Island Sound*. Netflix, 2021.

Growing up as I did in Connecticut, the start of August brought with it an annual tradition for my family: a getaway that consisted of renting a small apartment on Block Island for a week. A part of Rhode Island, Block Island is a potato-shaped piece of land located to the south of the mainland state, to the east of Long Island, and to the west of Martha's Vineyard, and I would cherish those trips for their combination of swimming, bicycling, and reading on the beach. It was our Block Island trip when I was twenty that holds a special place in my life, as it was on that trip that I first read H. P. Lovecraft. In particular, I remember one clammy, fog-shrouded evening, when the rest of the family had gone to sleep, that I first read "The Shadow over Innsmouth" and felt transported to that other New England seaside town. It was the atmosphere of that Block Island evening in which I read it that still causes me to consider "Innsmouth" to be Lovecraft's most effectively tense story. Years later, when I finally read Lovecraft and R. H. Barlow's "The Night Ocean," I was immediately taken back to nocturnal moonlit walks along Block Island's Crescent Beach. Imagine my shock when, reading through the *Selected Letters,* I found that both Lovecraft and Barlow were descended from among the first English settlers of Block Island (*Selected Letters* 4.337; Joshi, *I Am Providence* 980; Faig 195).

Several years ago, I tried—largely to no avail—to determine whether there was a deeper connection between Lovecraft and Block Island, the result of which I published in the island's local newspaper. Lovecraft does occasionally mention Block Island in letters and essays, for example showing awareness of the island's pioneering transatlantic radio broadcast towers of the early 1900s (*Selected Letters* 4.65) and beginning his essay "Some Dutch Footprints in New England" with the account of the island's naming for Dutch sailor Adriaen Block (*Collected Essays* 4.253). Block Island also has a history of folk legends—particularly the Palatine Lights, the supposed specters of a 1738 shipwreck—that Lovecraft almost certainly was familiar with; they were published in a book Lovecraft owned, Charles M. Skinner's *Myths and Legends of our Own Land* (1896), appearing immediately after the entries on Connecticut legends that Lovecraft incorporated into "The Dunwich Horror" (Joshi and Schultz, *Lovecraft's Library* 167; Skinner 241–48; Joshi, *I Am Providence* 411–12nn16–17).

Since Lovecraft's death, Block Island has been home to several other events that might have been of interest to the author. At the very end of World War II, the German submarine *U-853* was sunk off the island's coast, with human remains occasionally being removed from it in the years since (shades of *U-29* from "The Temple"). In 1996, the remains of an unidentified serpentine sea creature were recovered. Termed the "Block Ness Monster," its true nature will forever remain a mystery, as the bones were stolen in strange circumstances shortly thereafter (perhaps taken by the federal government to the same detention center for its prior Deep One arrests?). A 2017 German-language novel, *Lovecraft Letters* by Christian Gailus, appears to include a scene where Lovecraft visits the island in late 1936; but linguistic barriers hamper my ability to read it, and from my research it seems that any visit of the Old Gentleman to Block Island remains solely in the realm of fiction.[1] But an actual take on Block Island in a work of Lovecraftian horror? That appeared to linger only in my imagination—at least until March 11, 2021. On that day, Netflix released the horror movie *The Block Island Sound,* set and filmed on the island in spring 2018 and premiering at the Fantasia International Film Festival in August 2020.

The film revolves around the Lynch family. Father Tom, a fisherman, lives on Block Island with his unemployed son, Harry, while daughter Audry lives on mainland Rhode Island with

---

1. I have not, however, looked into whether Barlow ever visited his ancestral home.

her own daughter, Emily. With tourist season ending with the start of autumn, the population of Block Island plummets. As a result, Tom and Harry increasingly turn to drinking to pass the time.[2] After one evening passed in this way, Tom wakes up on his fishing boat, adrift in the eponymous body of water, with signs of fish and other objects seemingly dropped from the sky onto the deck. A rash of mass fish deaths causes EPA employee Audry to come study the phenomenon, staying with Tom and Harry and bringing Emily with her. The cause of the fish deaths stumps Audry, who tells Emily that she will have to take a few living fish to study; it might seem unkind to remove them from their homes, but it is only by studying them that the wider population can be helped. And in any case, most of the fish taken will be returned eventually.

While Audry may not know the cause of the deaths, Harry's drinking buddy Dale (who, as played by Jim Cummings, closely resembles *Re-Animator*–era Jeffrey Combs) suggests a number of conspiracy theories, including a toxoplasmosis-like parasite carried by an unknown sea monster. The visit comes with its own tension, as the heavy-drinking Tom behaves increasingly erratically, including vanishing on his boat in the middle of the night and frightening Emily. After one such night Tom does not return, and his boat is found empty, with apparent signs of a struggle and the radio receiving nothing but an unintelligible sound. When Tom's battered body is found on the beach the next day, Harry refuses to believe it was an accident, becoming erratic in the same manner as Tom, falling victim to mood swings and blackouts. Taking scuba gear from Audry's EPA site, Henry dives to the location where Tom's boat was discovered, only to become overwhelmed by an ink-like cloud, awakening hours later on the deck of the boat.

---

2. Tom and Harry's drinks of choice are repeatedly shown to be the beers of Providence-based Narragansett Brewing Company, founded the year of Lovecraft's birth. Appropriately, Narragansett both has a Lovecraft-themed line of beers and is a sponsor of NecronomiCon Providence. A can of Narragansett is also the beer drunk and crushed by fisherman Quint in the infamous scene in *Jaws,* another horror film set on a New England island.

Harry begins to see visions of Tom, who tells him to collect various objects—including the neighbor's dog—to bring to the same point in the ocean. When Harry does so, both he and the dog are taken into the sky, only for Harry to be dropped back down. Audry, meanwhile, has been consulting with a psychologist in Providence, who suggests that she talk with one of her former patients, now residing off the grid in West Greenwich.[3] The patient explains how the same thing happening to Henry happened to him in the past: a seemingly extraterrestrial presence compelling him to collect various objects to be lifted up into space. At the same time, the Tom avatar returns again to Henry, telling him that the aliens now demand a "girl."

Henry tries to resist but ultimately succumbs, kidnapping Emily just as Audry returns, taking all three of them to the point on the Block Island Sound where the aliens gather their collections for study. Audry is unable to awaken Henry from his torpor, but she manages to secure Emily from being lifted out of the boat's cabin, even as both Audry and Henry are taken away. Emily is rescued by the Coast Guard; as the voice clip of Audry's earlier explanation to her daughter about the need to sample fish for study to learn how to protect them is played, the movie ends with Audry being shown being dropped back into the sea from out of the sky.

To state the obvious, having a horror film centered around both the sea and unknown extraterrestrial intervention that is set in Rhode Island will invite comparisons to Lovecraft. This is clear in the reviews of *The Block Island Sound* that came out of its Fantasia debut. Said reviewers, however, are split on whether the comparison holds up. One argues that the film

> mines the region's close association with the uncanny, wriggling mythology of HP Lovecraft. . . . This is a truly cosmic horror story with some unnerving implications about man's place in the universe, but it functions just as well as a remarkably grounded character study. The real story here is as much about the tensions within the Lynch clan as it is about elder gods. (Goff)

---

3. Perhaps ironically, it was to the region that is now West Greenwich that Lovecraft's ancestors relocated after leaving Block Island (Faig 32n52).

Another reviewer diametrically counters, beginning by establishing the movie as "the rare horror story that deals with inhuman mysteries on the northeastern coast of the United States while not feeling Lovecraftian at all" (Surridge). To that reviewer, the anti-Lovecraftian sentiment is twofold: one is the plot (focusing on family and class in a way he argues Lovecraft tended not to) and the other is "that the look and feel of the film is also different from the twice-told narrative frame-structures of so much of Lovecraft." A third reviewer, however, helpfully splits the difference, defining the film as "A little bit of HP Lovecraft infused storytelling. . . . Except . . . it's not. But it is!" (Kautzer).

In a very strict sense this is not a Lovecraft film, in that it is not based on a work of Lovecraft nor has a callback to any of his works, outside of the single reference to Providence. The creatures responsible for manipulating the Lynch family are given no name, let alone ones consisting of the stereotypical strings of consonants and apostrophes. There are even fewer (i.e., no) tentacles or fish-human hybrids than in *The Lighthouse,* the prior indie horror movie set on a New England island. But is it *Lovecraftian?* Even Surridge's review does not deny this, specifically stating that it does not *feel* Lovecraftian. Whether it feels Lovecraftian is a personal matter; I for one would argue with him that issues of family or class are absent in Lovecraft's work, let alone in his voluminous letters. That the narrative structure is different from anything Lovecraft wrote is harder to deny, but I would also argue that it is meaningless. Compare "The Shadow over Innsmouth," *The Case of Charles Dexter Ward,* and *The Dream-Quest of Unknown Kadath:* how similar are those three, let alone a random sample of Lovecraftian pastiches from August Derleth, Ramsey Campbell, or Caitlín R. Kiernan?

I would argue that the lack of direct references to Lovecraft's fiction only adds to the Lovecraftian feel of the movie. If the Lynch family were renamed the Olmsteads and the setting relocated to Massachusetts, *The Block Island Sound* could almost serve as a direct sequel to "Innsmouth"; similarly, if set in rural Vermont and the family renamed the Akeleys, it could have been a take on "The Whisperer in Darkness." That it does not go down those tracks is to the film's credit; it can explore the similarities in themes and tones to those Mythos staples while charting its own course, without being bound to following either the plot specifics or the expectations that such a sense of continuity would have left. Similarly, the theme of shadowy horror emerging in a New England seaside resort town as tourism season ends is also central to "The Night Ocean," though in recent years it has become accepted that Barlow was responsible for the majority of that work.

However, outside of Lovecraft specifically, there is one Lovecraft-adjacent work that *The Block Island Sound* clearly draws from: Charles Fort's 1919 compilation of strange factoids, *The Book of the Damned*. In the book's introduction to the chapter on astronomy is Fort's famous speculation on humans' relation to extraterrestrials, "I think we're property." That sentence is preceded by a longer setup that tends not to be included with its conclusion, comparing humans with fish and aliens with the fishermen above, whose lures and reasoning alike are inscrutable to the fish:

> But what would a deep-sea fish learn even if a steel plate of a wrecked vessel above him should drop and bump him on the nose? Our submergence in a sea of conventionality of almost impenetrable density. Sometimes I'm a savage who has found something on the beach of his island. Sometimes I'm a deep-sea fish with a sore nose. (Fort 154–57)

The Book of the Damned was read and appreciated by Lovecraft (*Selected Letters* 2.174). He in turn adapted Fort's concept in his poem "The Outpost," in the form of the Fishers from Outside, who "found the worlds of old, And took what pelf [spoils] their fancy spied" (*Ancient Track* 77–79). Lin Carter would later adapt the Fishers from Outside in a story of the same name, where all the nuance of Fort's original concept is removed in favor of turning them into stock *Call of Cthulhu*-fied eldritch entities who visited Earth to build ancient temples for cultists to worship them (Carter 46). The unseen antagonists (if they are even antagonists, given their direct comparison to EPA researchers trying to do what is best to preserve an endangered species) of *The Block Island*

Sound are a much more accurate take on both Fort's original idea and on the name Lovecraft gave to them, down to the parallel—so on the nose, it could not be a coincidence—of having island fishermen be their targets.

We are in a golden age of Lovecraftian pastiche, adaptation, and scholarship at the moment. But if there is one unique aspect of this particular Lovecraftian renaissance compared to earlier ones, it is that specific references to Lovecraft have become less important. Take for example *Lovecraft Country,* the HBO show that debuted two weeks before *The Block Island Sound,* and which made almost no direct use of Lovecraft beyond his name in the title, but still engaged in critiques of (some of) his broader themes. It is also far more Lovecraftian than the early 2020 film *Underwater,* an otherwise-typical action movie whose claim to the genre is the inclusion of an underwater monster at the end.

In this way, the argument over whether *The Block Island Sound* meets an arbitrary standard of "Lovecraftiness" is pedantic—although I do firmly think it is Lovecraftian, far more than most films (or, for that matter, written pastiches) that simply appropriate names from the Mythos. What is more important is that *The Block Island Sound,* for being a low-budget indie film, is very well made and combines both smaller-scale psychological horror with questions over the larger place of humanity in the cosmos, in a way that brings to mind the 2019 conspiracy culture throwback *The Vast of Night*. After the past year, it is also a stark reminder that the shutting down of blockbuster studio productions does not have to mean the end of quality movie output. For these reasons, I would heartily recommend *The Block Island Sound* to anyone seeking a horror/sci-fi film set on the shores of Rhode Island, in whatever genre of horror you feel most comfortable applying to it.

Works Cited

Carter, Lin. "The Fishers from Outside." *Crypt of Cthulhu* No. 54 (1988): 43–52.

Faig, Kenneth W., Jr. *The Unknown Lovecraft*. New York: Hippocampus Press, 2009.

Fort, Charles. *The Book of the Damned*. New York: Horace Liveright, 1919.

Goff, Oscar. "Fantasia Review: The Block Island Sound (2020) dir. The McManus Brothers." *Boston Hassle* (30 August 2020). bostonhassle.com/fantasia-review-the-block-island-sound-2020-dir-the-mcmanus-brothers/

Guimont, Edward. "H. P. Lovecraft and Block Island." *Block Island Times* 49, No. 9 (2 March 2019): 13.

Joshi, S. T. "Explanatory Notes." In H. P. Lovecraft. *The Thing on the Doorstep and Other Weird Stories*. Ed. S. T. Joshi. New York: Penguin, 2001. 367–443.

———. *I Am Providence: The Life and Times of H. P. Lovecraft*. New York: Hippocampus Press, 2010. 2 vols.

———, and David E. Schultz. *Lovecraft's Library: A Catalogue*. 4th rev. ed. New York: Hippocampus Press, 2017.

Kautzer, A. W. "The Block Sound Island—Fantasia Film Festival 2020." *The Movie Isle* (28 August 2020). themovieisle.com/2020/08/28/the-block-sound-island-fantasia-film-festival-2020/

Lovecraft, H. P. *The Ancient Track: Complete Poetical Works*. Ed. S. T. Joshi. 2nd ed. New York: Hippocampus Press, 2013.

———. *Collected Essays*. Ed. S. T. Joshi. New York: Hippocampus Press, 2004–06. 5 vols.

———. *Selected Letters*. Ed. August Derleth, Donald Wandrei, and James Turner. Sauk City, WI: Arkham House, 1965–76. 5 vols.

Skinner, Charles M. *Myths and Legends of Own Land*. Philadelphia: J. B. Lippincott Co., 1896.

Surridge, Matthew David. "Fantasia 2020, Part XXII: The Block Island Sound." *Black Gate* (22 September 2020). www.blackgate.com/2020/09/22/fantasia-2020-part-xxii-the-block-island-sound/

Ramsey's Rant: Dancing the Night Away

Ramsey Campbell

If this essay achieves nothing but to bring the film *Zinda Laash* to a wider audience, my mission on earth may be complete. It's a 1967 Pakistani film known variously in English as *The Living Corpse* and *Dracula in Pakistan*. While the first title is the closer translation, the latter title sums the film up best (though to confuse the issue, IMDb lists a 1986 film also known as *Zinda Laash* or *The Living Corpse*, by the sound of it a slice of life, not even undead). Although the 1967 release begins with Professor Tabani's bid to brew an immortality elixir, he's asleep in a coffin (which appears to offer a cloak as an accessory) before the opening credits roll, and soon his reign of terror is opposed by none other than vampire hunter Harker—Dr Aqil Harker, to be precise. Resemblances proliferate, not just to Stoker but to Terence Fisher's *Dracula,* from which it lifts images and entire sequences and music cues. Though the score is credited to Tassadaque Hussain, much of it consists of random chunks of James Bernard's soundtrack for the Fisher film with added tabla and, at the finale, resurrecting Christopher Lee's cries at the sunlight. *La Cucaracha* and several other jolly tunes are present throughout too. Most unforgettable is the recreation of Valerie Gaunt's attack on John van Eyssen. Whereas Gaunt merely pleads for help before biting her victim, her Pakistani counterpart performs an entire seductive dance (cut by the domestic censor at the time) and not to Bernard's music either. Instead she's accompanied by Hank Marvin and the Shadows, I imagine very much to their surprise, performing *Peace Pipe*. The film has a great deal more to offer the unwary, and writing about it has driven me to repeat the experience. Meanwhile I'm prompted to reflect on how often dance is an element in horror and allied films, nowhere more so than at the end of Pasolini's *Saló,* where it represents inhuman indifference.

I don't have so much in mind sedate occasions that are invaded by the monstrous—the masked ball in Lon Chaney's *Phantom of the Opera,* for instance, though that doesn't involve much dance. I'm thinking more of dance that expresses or illuminates the central theme, not to mention quite a bunch of films where it seems to do nothing of the kind. Jungle monsters in particular can expect dancers to put on a show for them, however defensive. If King Kong is the prototype, this (like the film) may have been inspired by the infamous *Ingagi*, though its rampant apes aren't actually summoned by the simulated tribal gambols. In *From Hell It Came* dancers wiggle their grass skirts at their fellow tribesman whose execution, together with some handy atomic fallout, will turn him into the stumpy chap who does something like the title says. All these routines have some thematic relevance, but elsewhere dance seems to have settled into convention, becoming one of those things you do because you're in a fantastic film—keeping an ape in the cellar, or ignoring signs of your imminent demise, however ominous the location (although is this more conventionalised than, say, the troubadour Manrico singing how he must race to save his mother from the pyre, a mission so urgent he repeats the entire aria?). While these may claim to advance the narrative, it's harder to accord some dances that excuse. In an indulgent mood, I could lend one to *Cannibal Terror* (which even Jesus Franco might disown, although for years it was misattributed to him), in which the suspiciously European cannibals make a bid to demonstrate how primitive they are by jigging on the spot, some even managing to hide their mirth.

Dance is central to some films in our genres, of course. Michael Powell may have invited further outrage from those who professed themselves appalled by *Peeping Tom* when he made Moira Shearer perform a joyful dance before her death, but it's in her character, and the contrast is powerful—indeed, the scene can be viewed as the culmination of their collaborations, starting from the ballet that acts out the ballerina's obsessions in *The Red Shoes* and prefigures the tragic finale (invoking the horror of Hans Andersen's tale by association), and taking in Shearer's witty automaton turn as Coppelia in *Tales of Hoff-*

mann (which George Romero called "almost a horror film" and cited as the single greatest cinematic influence on his work). The remake of *Suspiria* integrates ballet with the narrative more closely than the original manages and offers the horrific set-piece of a dance that acts as sympathetic magic, all of which helps enliven the visual drabness of this version, though the overhead shots of the climactic dance invoke fancies of a macabre Busby Berkeley. *Audition* (the only horror film that Robin Wood found nearly impossible to watch, unless we admit *Saló* to the category) leaves us to decide whether Asami's revengeful psychosis has its roots in the dance tuition she suffered as a child, but there's no doubt how gruelling such tuition is. No film renders ballet and its demands more nightmarish than *Black Swan,* incidentally a more disquieting treatment of maternal oppression than the reworking of *Suspiria.* All of this leaves me unsurprised that ballet training sometimes leads or allies itself to BDSM, not least for stars of the genre—Leia Ann Woods and Ariel Anderssen come immediately to my mind. Indeed, Ariel confirms it, telling me that the training is "superbly masochistic" and that "dancers don't get treated like adults & everybody shouts at them". It seems Maria Ouskenspaya's fearsome matriarch who runs the ballet school in *Waterloo Bridge* isn't so exaggerated after all, and we may recollect that the "Good Morning" scene in *Singin' in the Rain* took twelve hours to shoot, after which Debbie Reynolds had to be carried off the set, unable to walk.

The horror musical is a territory in itself, and somewhat apart from my theme. I can't let *The Rocky Horror Picture Show* pass unmentioned—for my money its true coup is casting Charles Gray as the narrator, incidentally according him a few steps of the Timewarp, a spectacle as comically unsettling as the sight of Christopher Walken performing a dance. Gray's greatest contribution to our field was his Mocata in *The Devil Rides Out,* Colin McCourt's musical version of which is represented on YouTube. Jerome Sable's *Stage Fright* deserves a special mention for succeeding—certainly for me—as both a musical and a slasher film, while de Palma's *Phantom of the Paradise* takes a similarly parodic course. Like Argento's twin variations on the phantom's famous tale, even when the music isn't operatic, de Palma's style here can be said to be.

How thematically crucial are the background dances in *Midsommar*? Like much of the film (not least the psychedelic episode, the most disquieting depiction of a trip I've ever seen) they convey a sense of surreptitious wrongness, rather as I find in similar images in the work of Miklós Jancsó. *Dance of the Vampires* is named for its powerful finale, which is just one of the episodes that straddle horror and dark comedy. Don Sharp's *Kiss of the Vampire* (not by any means to be mistaken for Joe Tornatore's film that adopted the same name) uses a masked ball to lure the heroine into the villain's clutches. Which film may the ballroom scene in A *Cure for Wellness* seek to invoke?

The teen monster films of the fifties—whether the supposed teenagers are themselves monstrous or simply there to be chased or to know better than the adults in town—generally feature a Twist, if not a twist, or some similar dance. Perhaps because its Christian creators aimed to be positive about youngsters, *The Blob* contains no such sinful stuff. Often it's simply an interlude, sometimes—as in *Frankenstein's Daughter*—as hilarious as the rest of the film. In *Sting of Death,* the dance the assembled teens perform to Neil Sedaka's "Do the Jellyfish" might well be seen as sufficient provocation for the monster—a chap with a plastic bag on his head—to sting every one of them. In *Earth vs. the Spider,* the high school hop shakes the giant spider out of its torpor and sends it on a rampage, although it spares the rock band. I gather spiders have no ears.

We might expect no dance to be more thematically crucial than the climactic scene of *The Masque of the Red Death,* and indeed it is, since the crimson intruder infects the guests not just with the plague but with a compulsion to dance out their deaths. Sadly, it's a perfunctory performance that Roger Corman wished he'd had more time to stage, but at least it doesn't try to emulate the iconic image of Death's parade that bears off the knight and his companions in *The Seventh Seal,* a film to which Corman's owes other ideas. Despite Dr Phibes' disfigurement, Vincent Price has a better time waltzing with Vulnavia, a routine that lends him some humanity. Antonio

Margheriti's *Danza Macabra* evokes the uncanny with a glimpse of ghostly dancers in a distant room. Most haunting are the ballroom dances in *Carnival of Souls*, a memorably spectral vision.

Dance rarely grows violent, except against its performer, though there is the extraordinary terpsichorean rape enactment in Michele Soavi's *Stage Fright,* perhaps not quite so startling if we remember the choreographed leadup to a near-rape in Robert Wise's *West Side Story*. In the South Korean *Wishing Stairs* a student shoves her friend down them to ensure herself a place in a ballet school, but the extensive ballet sequences are far less haunted than they deserve to be. Gaspar Noé's *Climax* fragments the vigorous choreography of its opening minutes to stage a hellish hallucinated descent into chaos. In some senses it's the ultimate treatment of our theme. The cast consists entirely of dancers, and the film was improvised without a script or preconceived routines. It celebrates the combined talents of its performers so persuasively that the ensuing bedlam is all the more horrific. Noé greatly admires Kubrick, and yet his own methods are close to the opposite of Kubrick's, whose rigorousness may be epitomised by *Full Metal Jacket*'s gruelling choreography.

I'm approaching the end of this haphazard survey. Does *Zinda Laash* have any real competitors? You could make a triple bill of three hilarious fifties science fiction films, or at least their dance interludes. In *Cat-Women of the Moon* the titular ladies perform a rite accompanied by a timid tango, while their solitary counterpart in the remake *Missile to the Moon* has to make do with bongo drums and castanets (not to mention a giant spider recycled from the original), but *Fire Maidens from Outer Space* has the edge for overload, since the Borodin tunes that accompany most of the action eventually drive one lady and then several to prance demurely in three separate scenes. Honourable mention if no more is due to the arachnid lady's routine in *Mesa of Lost Women,* performed to a (to put it kindly) improvisational score so memorable that Ed Wood, no less, recycled it in *Jail Bait*. More fun is to come, but before I reveal the shortlist I see I've overlooked two splendid displays that need no special pleading—Britt Eklund's magically erotic dance in *The Wicker Man* and Rihanna's transformative stage routine in *Valerian and the City of a Thousand Planets,* both joyous in their different ways. My final candidates may bring you joy as well, if your tastes are as outré as mine.

If only the 1990 Bollywood production *Bandh Darwaza* gave its vampire a song and dance to perform! The experience would be complete. As it stands, his possibly undead daughter gets to bewail her lot in song and momentarily dance with his shadow. In some ways a timid sort, the vampire tends to run away from threats and bash his way through walls rather than going around. He likes to advertise, as witness his travelling hearse decorated with a giant skull and crossbones. At least his helpers alert him to the presence of a victim with a dance. Still, I may award the palm to *She Demons,* if only for a quintessential demonstration of how tropes of the genre persist well past any motivation. When the female dance troupe kept in cages on a tropical island by a Nazi scientist (who turns them into fanged monsters as a side effect of his bids to beautify his disfigured wife) manage to escape, they build a fire in a glade a few hundred yards away and dance in celebration of their freedom to drums that contrive to sound like a jazz orchestra. Top that if you can, Ed Wood! Certainly if you've enjoyed Wood's films, the work of Richard Cunha will reward you too. It would be remiss of me not to spread the good word.

(Special thanks to John Llewellyn Probert and Thana Niveau for suggestions)

An Old-World Rarity Reissued

Peter Cannon

CASSIE SYMMES. *Old World Footprints.* Edited and annotated by David Goudsward. N.p.: Bold Venture Press, 2021. 58 pp. $9.95 tpb. ISBN 9798710253847.

At the center of this slender volume are the two "unremarkable travelogues," as Goudsward, the author of *H. P. Lovecraft in the Merrimack Valley,* calls them in his introduction, that Cassie Symmes, Frank Belknap Long's maternal aunt, had privately printed in 1928 in an edition of 300 copies as *Old World Footprints*. The publisher was W. Paul Cook's Recluse Press, and the preface was signed Frank Belknap Long, Jr., though it was in fact ghostwritten by H. P. Lovecraft. As such, this is one of the most obscure bits of prose HPL published in his lifetime, if also one of the least significant. In a letter to Clark Ashton Smith the next year, he refers to it as a "euphemistic hash." For once, Lovecraft wasn't being too modest.

Of far more interest than the two short travel pieces, "England" and "Switzerland, Italy, and the Mediterranean," is Goudsward's biographical essay, "Cassie Symmes, Inadvertent Lovecraftian," an earlier version of which ran in the *Lovecraft Annual* No. 9 (2015). She was born Cassie Mansfield Doty in 1872, in Bayonne, N.J.; she was her sister May's maid of honor when May married Dr. Frank Long in 1891; and she married sixty-six-year-old William B. Symmes, Sr., a prosperous New York produce wholesaler, in 1917. In subsequent years, the couple frequently traveled to Europe and Florida. Symmes, whose health was in decline, died in Manhattan in 1928, around the time *Old World Footprints* was in production, and it fell on Lovecraft to do the proofreading, which may well account for why the text includes some archaic spellings and terms. Cassie herself was killed in a motor accident in Florida in 1935.

This attractively produced book is illustrated with period postcards and photographs, as well as a facsimile of the original title page. Pulp scholar Bobby Derie contributes a lively foreword, and a concluding essay, "Lovecraft on Symmes," cites passages from Lovecraft's letters related to her and the publication of *Old World Footprints*. Bold Venture Press deserves much credit for reissuing this rare collector's item in an affordable trade edition. I for one was fascinated by all the new information about the extended Long family, and I hope Goudsward will in due course draw on his extensive research to produce a full biography of Frank Belknap Long.

Weird Fiction, Weird Musick

Oliver Sheppard

I have upon me the somewhat rare cassette issue of punk band Rudimentary Peni's sprawling *Cacophony* LP, which was released to mixed reviews—and much confusion in the underground music press—in 1988. Much has been written of H. P. Lovecraft's influence on music since the 1960s, starting usually with the actual band that named itself "H. P. Lovecraft," formed in the late 1960s. They were a psych-folk act, but it is Lovecraft's influence on metal that is nowadays most widely known. Until now, no one has really written an extensive history of perhaps weird fiction's most obsessive—and I do mean obsessive—music group, Rudimentary Peni.

Rudimentary Peni's *Cacophony* is an H. P. Lovecraft tribute album that seems to have been made on a mixture of absinthe, LSD, and amphetamines. Standing at a monstrous thirty-one tracks (depending on what you count as an individual "track," since many of the tracks blend into one another or are spoken-word fragments), it has been compared to the Beatles' *White Album* in its ambition, but also in its unevenness. Above, I mention the cassette version of *Cacophony* because it is the only version whose cover contains an illustration by award-winning artist Nick Blinko of Lovecraft's story "The Music of Erich Zann." Of course, Nick Blinko is also the singer of Rudimentary Peni (who are a trio), and he does all the band's artwork; and on the cassette version of *Cacophony* we see the elderly, mute Erich Zann floating out his garret window, viola in hand, drifting away into the maw of a carnivorous void.

Rudimentary Peni released *Cacophony* on their own label, Outer Himalayan Records, itself a vague Lovecraftian reference intended to evoke images of the Plateau of Leng. Five years earlier, the band had released the now-legendary *Death Church* LP on Corpus Christi Records, a side-imprint of Crass Records. Incredibly, that album reached #3 in the UK Indie Charts. *Death Church* was a doomy album, too; but, given its proximity to the anarcho-punk scene of that time, it was also very political. Big things were expected from Rudimentary Peni's follow-up LP. But after *Death Church,* there was only silence. For five years.

Then—*Cacophony*. *Cacophony* does not announce itself as a Lovecraft concept album at any point. You either figure that out for yourself or you don't. And many didn't. "Career suicide," came many responses. "What on earth . . ." were others.

Every song on *Cacophony* has something to do with Lovecraft's life or fiction. The track "Kappa Alpha Tau," for example, refers to the gang of cats Lovecraft tended to. (The acronym "K.A.T." was Lovecraft's clever designation for the feline fraternity he cared for.) The haunting, excellent song "The Only Child" refers to Lovecraft's mother treating the young horror writer as a little girl, going so far as to dress him up in girls' gowns and grow his hair long while cruelly reminding him she had always wanted a girl instead of a boy. The shrieking, repetitive chorus of "I'm a little girl, I'm a little girl!" is indeed jarring. And "The Old Man Is Not So Terribly Misanthropic," as another example, refers to Lovecraft's transformation from an early reactionary supporter of racial eugenics to an advocate of a type of New Deal-ian "aristocratic socialism" (in Peni's lyrics) before his death. Most of *Cacophony's* references can be figured out by reading L. Sprague de Camp's biography of Lovecraft, which is sort of the cipher for the entire LP. (In fact, I bought a copy of de Camp's *Lovecraft: A Biography* off Mr. de Camp himself shortly before I bought *Cacophony* on cassette in 1991 or so, and *Cacophony* basically plays out like the audio version of that biography.)

Often, *Cacophony's* songs are strung together with spoken-word bits: Blinko reciting a critic's condemnation of Lovecraft ("Howard was a twitch, boys and girls, and that's all there is to it!"); band members making distorted noises intended to make one think of gibbering shoggoths; a recitation of all the pen names Lovecraft ever used (including a sly reference to Poe's Zoilus); a list of other authors who inspired Lovecraft (M. R. James, Hawthorne, Poe, etc.); and a definition of digestive cancer, which ultimately killed Lovecraft. In the spoken-word track "Better Not Born," Blinko recites from

Lovecraft's suicide confession, relayed via his voluminous correspondence:

"How easy it would be to wade out among the rushes and lie face down in the warm water till oblivion came. There would be a certain gurgling or choking unpleasantness at first—but it would soon be over. Then the long, peaceful night of non-existence . . ."

The overall opus that is *Cacophony* could be described as a sprawling, moody, quirky, and slightly insane monstrosity punctuated with bits of speedy punk rock here and there tempered with slower, more melodic punk rock odes elsewhere. I can't think of another '80s punk album to compare it to.

In the 1990s, Blinko took his own turn at writing weird fiction, of a sort, with his novel *Primal Screamer,* recently reprinted by PM Press. The original copy on Spare Change Press fetches a ton of money on used-book markets nowadays. And to be frank, *Primal Screamer* is a mixed affair. It is a thinly veiled autobiographical novel of Blinko himself, told from the standpoint of his therapist, with supernatural elements thrown in. Later, Blinko illustrated a stand-alone edition of Lovecraft's "Pickman's Model," which also fetches high prices on eBay and elsewhere.

In the meantime, Blinko's status as an outsider artist has garnered him more acclaim, ironically, than the music of his band. David Tibet of post-industrial band Current 93 started working with Blinko in the 2000s around the time he (Tibet) also began to work with Thomas Ligotti—and here is where occurs another incredibly important intersection between weird music and weird fiction. Tibet's own Strange Attractor Press has recently been aided by MIT in putting forth reprints of assembled occult, weird, and other various supernatural, or apocalyptic fiction—including works by Ligotti, Lovecraft, Clark Ashton Smith, and related authors. Tibet's working with both Nick Blinko and Thomas Ligotti has succeeded in sowing together a lot of disparate milieus that before seemed irreconcilable.

As many know, Blinko was confined against his will in an insane asylum in the early 1990s under Section 3 of the UK Mental Health Act of 1983 due to hallucinations that he was

Pope Adrian IV, brought on by his recurrent schizoaffective disorder. These hallucinations became the basis for the third Rudimentary Peni LP, *Pope Adrian 37th Psychristiatric*, released in 1995 although recorded in 1992. This was another concept LP, and Rudimentary Peni's first LP after the Lovecraftian *Cacophony* album. In the meantime, the Henry Boxer Gallery in London began to exhibit Blinko's art as outsider art; and Colin Rhodes, in the Thames & Hudson book *Outsider Art: Spontaneous Alternatives* (2000), began noting Blinko as an important outsider artist, noting:

> In the case of British artist Nick Blinko (b. 1961), who has in the past been hospitalised, the need to make pictures is stronger than the desire for the psychic 'stability' brought by therapeutic drugs which adversely affects his ability to work. His images are constructed of microscopically detailed elements, sometimes consisting of literally hundreds of interconnecting figures and faces, which he draws without the aid of magnifying lenses and which contain an iconography that places him in the company of the likes of Bosch, Bruegel and the late Goya. These pictures produced in periods when he was not taking medication bring no respite from the psychic torment and delusions from which he suffers. In order to make art, Blinko risks total psychological exposure.

David Tibet's Strange Attractor Press has also started reprinting Nick Blinko's artwork as well as his writing, including *The Haunted Head* in 2009, when Tibet's publishing arm was called Coptic Cat Press. And in 2020, Blinko was awarded the Grand Prix of the prestigious "Triennial of Self-Taught Visionary Art" at Belgrade in February 2020, one of Europe's premier outsider art awards.

The question remains: will the singer of punk band Rudimentary Peni, an acclaimed outsider artist, continue to write fiction? Has Rudimentary Peni, in fact, written the music of Erich Zann? Only time will tell. But it is important to keep in mind this prescient quotation from Thomas Ligotti:

> Let's say it once and for all: Poe and Lovecraft—not to mention a Bruno Schulz or a Franz Kafka—were what the world at large would consider extremely disturbed individuals. And

most people who are that disturbed are not able to create works of fiction. These and other names I could mention are people who are just on the cusp of total psychological derangement. Sometimes they cross over and fall into the province of "outside aritists." That's where the future development of horror fiction lies—in the next person who is almost too emotionally and psychologically damaged to live in the world but not too damaged to produce fiction.

Bedlam's Children

Michael D. Miller

WILLIAM HOLLOWAY. *Blackwood Estates*. Carbondale, IL: JournalStone Publishing, 2020. 146 pp. $18.95 tpb. ISBN: 9781950305483.

Let me introduce you to *Blackwood Estates,* a novel of cosmic horror, straight no chaser, from William Holloway. The work itself is a short, high-paced narrative taking place over two days, and told with an urgency making the novel readable in that amount of time or less, confirming certainly Poe's idea that the unity-of-effect is best had in one sitting (or possibly two, in this case).

Blackwood Estates is set in an imaginary suburb outside of Austin, Texas, visited upon by a cosmic apocalyptic event. We experience the story through Phil Nada, a recently separated father of Scotty, his autistic son, and owner of Benny, his dog and last true friend. Phil is also a writer of horror, giving his experience an apparent irony of sorts. In a short introduction to his life and his suburban seclusion, featuring occupants like "White Escalade Blonde from over by the Trails" and "Prius Latina in Reflector Shades Listening to Metallica," we are hit right away in the first chapter with a disastrous incident. There is a strange sound, followed by a smell, and then a disturbance in the air. Very soon the children of Blackwood Estates are acting violent, attacking neighbors, parents, torturing innocent cats, overtly making the demon-possessed doll Chucky seem quite tame. Incidentally, Scotty is also possessed in like manner, leaving Phil, Benny and a few neighbors, to find a way to save the children and Blackwood Estates while contending with the environment around them drying up by the minute. Holloway then takes us through each incremental incident in short moving chapters until its doom-fulfilling conclusion thirty-three chapters later.

The cosmic event in this story is threefold. The big event is that a coterie of inmates from the Bedlam Asylum circa 1890 led by one Louis Villefort have executed an occult ritual to transport them out of the asylum and setting them free on the other side of the Thames. The second event is that Blackwood Estates has a dark occultist of its own, one Lloyd Reynolds, Esq., an aging, retired lawyer who by night slips into "the place" (also known as the space between spaces) via a combination of black widow spider venom and sacrificing children. It so happens these rituals accidentally cross over each other and the Bedlam inmates' minds are transplanted into the children of Blackwood Estates (being that is the location of Lloyd's self-created dimensional gate to "the place"). Lloyd's mess-up has prevented him from attaining permanent transfer to "the space between the spaces" and he is out to finish what he started. Louis Villefort, in the body of Scotty, once learning of the mishap, seeks to undo the cosmic accident, but must gather his fellow inmates, now assembled like a mad zombie herd on the suburban streets. Phil himself is caught between these forces, the vile actions of Louis and his love for Scotty, while a bigger annihilating threat hunts them all.

The servitors of both rituals of Louis and Lloyd require payment in blood; and as these rituals were undone, this has unleashed the Hunters of the Outer Dark upon Blackwood Estates, lapping up residents for their blood price. Phil, Scotty, and what few residents remain are cast into the chaos of all the events. The rift in the fabric of normalcy, "the Sublimity," has also undone the laws of nature itself, the smell, the air, the heat, all the water being sucked out of everything while the characters attempt to undo the carnage. As with any true cosmic horror of the Lovecraftian type, we know there is no out, and all these actions to save the world are subject to time. And so, with great pacing and narrative, the space-time continuum will right itself, a moment known as "the Erasure." Caught between his son and Louis Villefort, Lloyd's machinations, and inevitable destruction, Phil is forced to confront the message of the cosmos itself, as the events take their course, despite the valiant efforts of humanity.

Author William Holloway has been known for such dark

bleak cosmic fiction. He published three novels with Horrific Tales UK, *Lucky's Girl* (2014), *The Immortal Body* (2015), and *Song of the Death God* (2017) of similar scope, and with Journalstone he contributed and edited the popular *Abyssal Plain: The R'lyeh Cycle*. William certainly puts the "A" in apocalyptic cosmic horror, so I decided to speak with him for a short time to discuss what this all means for *Blackwood Estates* and his body of work.

MM: So what is William Holloway's philosophy? Your authorial viewpoint expressed in your work?

WH: I was born a Nihilist. But I do not fully embrace that aspect of myself. I do believe that life can be a good thing, that joy can be experienced. That is what makes life worthwhile. While I know there is no point . . . I don't seek to cultivate it personally. It's there but I try not to feed it. Some people say, "resentment is like a stray dog, if you feed it, it will stick around." This is a dog that came with the house, so I have to be very careful not to overfeed it or it takes over the yard and drives away the neighbors.

MM: Many people associate cosmicism or the cosmic in horror with Lovecraft's comment "life is a hideous thing," meaning we get this nihilistic uncaring universe versus the "earth-gazing" route other writers take making humans much more central and important to the narrative. *Blackwood Estates* puts us in between those two paradigms, I think.

WH: *Blackwood Estates* is my lightest, least dark story. Generally, people attribute my worldview to a quotation from *Song of the Death God*. This is the one where people say ah, Bill is a Nihilist. Here's the passage: "To say that Carsten's desire to escape, to transcend, was exclusively due to his upbringing would be a mistake. He possessed a singular disgust with life, with the very concept of existence, the coming into being, the living as a stupid filthy animal, and the dying as a stupid filthy animal. For all his art and letters, man was still a form of slime, not all that different from his own excrement in the long view."

MM: Negative views of Nihilism, believing in nothing as many people define it, permeate our culture. Even if popular in many Lovecraft or Ligotti stories, it still puts many readers off. My students today always find the "no hope" aspect a let-down. Did you deal with the Texas setting, or the history of Bedlam,[4] in other stories? Is there a Holloway universe?

WH: Lloyd's character talks about "the accident" that caused him to be where he is. He talks about "a featureless stone place," THE PLACE, is a recurring feature in my stories. The Bardo from Buddhism, sort of. A central part of my "Singularity Cycle," which I consider to be my great work. It is far from finished, three books in. I can see why people think I'm a Nihilist with that one. It's dark. The upside is I write each novel in a different style and if there is one that's a little bit neo-noir it's that one.

MM: Is *Blackwood Estates* part of the cycle?

WH: It exists within the same universe.

MM: Is Bedlam or the Blackwood Estates unique to the cycle?

WH: The subdivision, Blackwood Estates, came from a name I thought was cool. Taken from author Algernon Blackwood and combined with estates. Then I thought, what is it? Etc. The story evolved from there. That's how my stories happen.

MM: The cover design, recalling some of the Michael Whelan 1980s Lovecraft covers, and the title certainly sold me. One thing about cosmic horror whether it is an event, like a meteor crashing to earth in "The Colour out of Space," or the opening of some dimensional gate between worlds, the philosophical concept of reality is changed, but you also tie that to physical things, the air being drained of moisture, the earth drying up into a husk, so the characters in *Blackwood Estates* have two dilemmas, the cosmic threat, via the Hunters of the

---

4. Notorious Bethlem Royal Hospital, first asylum for mentally ill in England, dating back to 1247.

Outer Dark, but their time is running out as well as the earth evaporates. You merge them together so there is an apocalyptic aftermath. When you look at cosmic horror stories, what would be your idea of how they work effectively?

WH: You don't have a singular antagonist, you have a catalyst which turns a place, the people, and everything else into a liminal space where anything can happen. I think THAT is partially what it's all about. There's this epistemic question too, what's all this about with cosmic horror? I know someone smarter than me might sum it up, but there is this idea that the scales are removed from your eyes and you see the universe for what it is and it's there to kill you. There's a band called Coil[5] whose song "Blood from the Air" is the most perfect encapsulation IN SOUND of cosmic horror that exists. In sound it's like the old adage about art and porn "you know it when you see it." Cosmic horror is kinda the same until somebody like a Joshi comes up with a better definition. Something happens and reveals the world to be a different thing than we thought. And a far more malevolent thing.

MM: One of the gravest aspects of cosmic horror to me, especially the Lovecraftian vein, is mind possession. The idea that from out of the depths of the universe some entity can take over another mind, rendering their identity and sense of consciousness null, is horrifying. You added another controversial element to it by having the children as the possessed in this case and the possessors turn them into killers. That's sure to upset a few detractors similar to Kinji Fukasaku's film *Battle Royal*.

WH: I am praised or ignored for that reason, kids and animals die in my stories. And people read to escape, and they don't want that and I respect that. It's innocence but that's the point. Innocence in cosmic horror has its own currency because bad people for instance are not sacrificed in black magic, good people are, because they are innocent.

---

5. Coil, English post-industrial band 1982–2004. You can listen to the song at www.youtube.com/watch?v=kP7BhDjB2WI

MM: Same could be said for many readers when they encounter cosmic horror. They are innocent of the way the universe works, especially apocalyptic cosmic horror. So what's next for William Holloway?

WH: I'm often incapable of writing anything that doesn't become this giant thing. Doing standalone stuff is not my strong suit.

MM: Would it be safe to say "The Singularity Cycle" isn't over?

WH: Oh, no. What's going to be happening is . . . *The Shadow Church*. That is book three of "The Singularity Cycle" [*The Immortal Body* and *Song of the Death God*]. It's dark.

So where does all this leave *Blackwood Estates* in the comparative world of weird fiction? The narrative style Holloway uses is very effective, but perhaps not always consistently controlled, yet makes the everyday "earth-gazing" tolerable. The narration speaks with the reader, a bit stream-of-consciousness as if Blackwood Estates were telling story as it knows the residents so well, sometimes talking to them in *italics*. This works at achieving a balance between the weirdness of the events and the characters. Lovecraft's own statement certainly applies: "I could not write about 'ordinary people' because I am not in the least bit interested in them. Without interest there can be no art. Man's relations to man do not captivate my fancy. It is man's relation to the cosmos—to the unknown—which alone arouses in me the spark of creative imagination. The human-centric pose is impossible for me, for I cannot acquire the primitive myopia which magnifies the earth and ignores the background." In short, the background is magnified in *Blackwood Estates,* but the characters are magnified in the narrative just enough to balance out this sentiment while staying true to cosmic horror.

Comparatively, this novel evokes from everywhere, it is *Village of the Damned* meets a cosmic event. It is *Invasion of the Body Snatchers* for children (or parents). It is Suburban Horror echoing *The House Next Door,* fusing the suburbia of *Edward Scissorhands* with *The Shining* . . .

> On the corner of Maypole and Bailey, they met the Smith twins, Denny and Penny . . . He [Phil] didn't know their parents, only that Dad drove a black Suburban and Mom drove a white Suburban . . . Ordinarily the only way you could tell them apart was the school uniforms, her in a plaid skirt and him in khaki pants and a tie. But there were no uniforms today, just shorts and t-shirts. Phil guessed the one in the pink was Penny and the one in the grey Transformers logo shirt was Denny.

Ironic enough they will be among the first transformed into Bedlam inmates.

With all the novel's cosmic calamity it manages to pack much modern thematic quality, terrorism, autism, parenting, children, father/son relationships, marriage, pet ownership, (a sort weird inverse of *I Am Legend* and "A Boy and His Dog"), mental illness, cannibalism, failing as man, father, husband, and the innocence of suburbia.

Blackwood Estates is in no way a pure pastiche of tales of cosmic horror; it is a continuation, a true descent of earlier menace. It echoes the expanding threat of the unknown similar to Frank Belknap Long's "The Space-Eaters" while being as pop culture relative and visually entertaining as the *Ash vs. Evil Dead* series. It has the immediacy of *Krampus* over two nights of horror—the threat is coming for you: "That night the Hunters of the Outer Dark came again, their foghorn whale songs splitting the firmament and separating the possessed from the possessors until all that was left were screaming, crying, and dying children . . . And they knew, too, that this death was just the beginning of their time in the terrible maw of their own hell." It is as if the best of the '70s horror paperbacks jumped ship to 2021. Far superior to Stephen King's *The Mist* or Josh Malerman's *Bird Box, Blackwood Estates* is dark, relentless, action-packed, cinematic, and worth a place in the canon of cosmic horror.

A Mexican Odyssey

Darrell Schweitzer

SILVIA MORENO-GARCIA. *Gods of Jade and Shadow*. London: Jo Fletcher Books, 2020. 336 pp. £8.99 tpb. ISBN 9781529402643.

Teenager Casiopea (spelled with one "s") Tun could readily identify with Cinderella, but explicitly refuses, even if she is treated as a poor relation by her maternal grandfather (who did not approve of her late father) and lorded over by her obnoxious and rather stupid cousin Martin. But Grandpa is a big man in the small Yucatan town where he lives almost like a feudal lord. How did he become so prosperous? It seems that he is a servant of the Maya death-god Vucub-Kamé, who is actually the usurping younger brother of the legitimate death god Hun-Kamé, who was reduced to a pile of bones that are stored in a locked box in Grandfather's bedroom. One day, when the rest of the household is off having fun and Casiopea is left to do the housework, she finds her grandfather's key and opens the box. Out pops Hun-Kamé in human form, but much diminished. To regain his power he must recover various bits of himself (an eye, a finger, an ear) that have been scattered about Mexico in the possession of various sorcerers and demons, all part of an elaborate strategy by his brother to lure him far away from his base of power in southern Mexico and to wear him down.

Hun-Kamé is wearing down too. It seems that a splinter of his bone is embedded in Casiopea's hand, enabling him to draw life from her, very slowly killing her. At the same time, as his nature merges with hers, he becomes less of a god, more of a mortal man, less and less able to confront his brother but capable of such things you would not expect in a death-god, such as smiling, or telling a joke, or generally experiencing a wider range of human emotions. Now Casiopea could free herself from this predicament by chopping her hand off, which would destroy the god and leave her maimed, or she could cooperate with him and hope for a reward should he regain his powers and win. It's 1927. The Jazz Age is in full swing. Casiopea has always wanted more out of life than servitude in a small Mexican town is likely to offer. So off she goes on a railway trip with a slightly shabby god, pursued by inept cousin Martin (who is working for Vucub-Kamé), encountering and sometimes battling other supernatural entities who have adjusted to modern life rather in the manner of those in Neil Gaiman's *American Gods*. Hun-Kamé isn't such a bad fellow, as far as death-gods go, but he is alarmed as he becomes more human and therefore weaker, even as Casiopea begins to fall in love with him. Should Vucub-Kamé win and defeat Hun-Kamé again, things will be very bad for both Casiopea and the world as a whole. Vucub-Kamé intends to restore the good old days and live on massive blood sacrifices.

I participated in a book discussion group that covered this book. Everybody found it very readable, having no difficulty following the unfamiliar Mayan mythology (a glossary is provided), but several complained that the book was "putdownable." That is, you could go on reading, or stop. It didn't seem to be all that compelling. I would say that I certainly wanted to finish it, but I would agree that it lacks intensity. The characters are real. We understand their emotions. But we are not made to care deeply. The actual level of literary skill here, the writing technique, is only about average. The strength of the book is the unfamiliar cultural perspective, both the mythological aspects and the depiction of Mexico in the 1920s. The author, who was born and raised in Mexico (but now lives in Canada), presumably knows what she is talking about. If she were an American, writing one more vampire or werewolf novel set in, say, New York, she wouldn't be very interesting, but coming from where she does, she gives fantasy fiction a new, distinct voice, and that *is* interesting. I will want to see more of her work.

Monsters Hidden in Plain Sight

June Pulliam

Them. Little Marvin, dir. 2021. Amazon.

If you do a Google search for Black horror, you are likely to find references to Jordan Peele's *Get Out,* as well as some lists of works by Black authors that include horrific elements. A list that I found on Penguin Random House's website admitted that "African American voices aren't well represented in horror literature" before leading into a list of works that are more science fiction, magical realism, or Gothic than what would be comfortably classified as horror. Three works from Penguin Random House's list include Toni Morrison's *Beloved,* Nnedi Okorafor's *Who Fears Death,* and Octavia Butler's *Fledgling*. The first two are examples of magical realism and science fiction respectively rather than horror. The horror genre is defined by the presence of a monster, but in Morrison's *Beloved* the ghost of the title is not viewed as monstrous by the community of former slaves she haunts because they view the supernatural as part of everyday life rather than something inherently monstrous. Even when Beloved breaks the family dog's jaw and saps the strength of her mother, she is not a monster so much as she is a traumatized soul. Nnedi Okorafor's novel, set in a post-apocalyptic future Sudan, is science fiction as much as it is horror. Okoafor is better known as a writer of speculative fiction and fantasy, and she is the winner of Hugo, Nebula, and World Fantasy Awards. Butler's *Fledgling,* about a new species of vampire who can walk in the daylight because of the melanin in her skin, is closer to horror. However, *Fledgling* is more concerned with the racism in the vampire community—several of their members want to destroy Shori, the lone Black vampire, merely because she is Black—than it is with the vampire as monster. And Butler too was a well-known science fiction writer.

Jordan Peele's *Get Out,* however, was not the first Black horror film, but its success prompted HBO to make a series out of Matt Ruff's novel *Lovecraft Country,* while Amazon released the new Black horror series *Them* in April of this year. These three works are crystallizing Black horror, which is so much more than horror created by Black authors and centering on Black characters. Amazon's *Them* tops them all.

Black horror is a bricolage of well-known horror tropes from what has been a predominantly white genre where monsters are racialized and sexualized Others. Black horror inverts these tropes to create an alternative universe viewed through a Black gaze to reveal monsters hiding in plain sight. For example, the first scene of Jordan Peele's *Get Out* opens with a young Black man walking through an upper middle-class suburb at night, searching for an address. This suburban setting viewed through the white gaze is a safe haven from danger, but the viewer sees this setting through the perspective of the nervous Black man who fears that someone will mistake him for a criminal and call the police. So, when a passing car slows down when it nears him, the viewer understands what it is like to be in this person's shoes. Later, when Chris is taken home to meet his girlfriend's wealthy white parents, he is uneasy even though they appear to be well-meaning white liberals. In fact, the girlfriend and her parents are monsters in ways that Chris could have never imagined before meeting them. *Lovecraft Country* views H. P. Lovecraft's tropes through a Black gaze. Lovecraft's racism is well known in works such as "Herbert West—Reanimator," where the mad scientist of the title discovers that non-whites (which included for him Italians) and poor whites, and even upper-class whites whose thinking is too contorted by Puritan morality lack the intellect to be reanimated as anything but terrifying creatures. *Lovecraft Country* blends the very real terrors of traveling while Black in the 1950s with Lovecraft's chthonic master race to reveal how the elite maintain power through racial and gendered hierarchies that keep entire classes of people of competing with them.

Little Marvin's *Them* builds on *Get Out* and *Lovecraft Country,* blending historical reality with the supernatural to create a work of horror that is not afraid to show the unspeakable. The Emory family is part of the Great Migration of Blacks who left the South to escape white violence, only to find more white violence in the North and the West. The Emorys move to Los Angeles and purchase a home in Compton, which is still primarily white in 1955. Henry Emory (Ashley Thomas) is persuaded to make this purchase sight unseen by a Los Angeles realtor who offers financing (in the 1950s, most banks would not give mortgages to Blacks). It is clear that the family members are not fully aware of what they are getting into when they arrive in Compton: they are greeted by glaring whites, who will later sit outside of the family's house day and night in an effort to drive them out, and they succeed after the family endures ten horrific days in the house. *Them* is filled with monsters, both natural and supernatural, and their monstrosity can only be recognized through the series' Black gaze. For example, Betty Wendell (Alison Pill), the leader of Compton's unofficial unwelcome wagon or white citizens council, could be mistaken for a sweet, submissive suburban wife. Or less obviously, Helen Koistra, the realtor who sold the home to the Emory family, and her business partners in the Southland Realty Corporation. Helen lures in families like the Emorys by telling them that the restrictive covenants on neighborhoods in places like Compton that prohibit owners to sell to "Negroes" are now illegal, which is true, but that detail won't stop Black families from being terrorized by their white neighbors who view the newcomers as responsible for driving down property values. The Southland Realty Corporation has weaponized white racism by deliberately selling homes to a few Black families, which drives the whites from the neighborhood, forcing them to sell their homes at a loss. The mortgages offered to Black families to purchase homes in Compton are on terms that almost guarantee that they will default: the interest rate is 20%, and the borrowers do not accrue equity in the homes as they pay off their notes. So if a family defaults, it loses both its home and all principal and interest it has paid, and the Southland Corporation will sell or rent the property to another Black family. If the family manages to pay off the mortgage and its usurious interest rate, the Southland Corporation also wins.

Sgt. Bull Williams is another monster hiding in plain sight. The Emory family dog is found dead in the basement on its second night in the home, prompting Lucky Emory (Deborah

Ayorinde) to grab her husband's service pistol and brandish it at the neighbors. The police arrive and threaten Henry with arrest, roughing him up in front of his terrified wife and children until Sgt. Williams arrives and tells the white neighbors to stop harassing the Emory family and then demands that his officers let Henry go. Sgt. Williams seems to be the one good member of the LAPD, but he is not motivated by any desire to enforce the law equally; instead, Sgt. Williams takes bribes from the Southland Corporation to discourage the Emory family from leaving in order to facilitate the company's blockbusting scheme.

The Emorys' experiences in South Carolina and Compton are not merely the result of some (a whole lot of) racist whites. Rather, they are due to systemic racism 400 years in the making in a country founded on slavery, colonization, and genocide. Lucky and her daughters are all haunted by versions of The Black Hat Man, the leader of a group of white colonists who enslave Lucky's ancestors. The Black Hat Man represents the pilgrims and other groups who migrated to North America in order to practice their faith freely. However, their own experiences being persecuted in the Old World did not persuade them to be tolerant and accepting of others. Instead, their dour Protestant faith justifies to them their dehumanization of Blacks. The Man in the Black Hat is a shapeshifter: he appears to young Gracie Emory as Miss Vera, a stern old schoolmistress who metes out brutal punishments to those who violate obscure rules, and to the teenaged Ruby Emory as Doris, the one white girl who will be her friend. Ruby's experience in her formerly all-white high school is similar to what Ruby Bridges experienced: white peers jeering at her for merely existing while teachers do not even attempt to intervene. Doris is the only girl in the school that Ruby can talk to, and so she is unaware of how this friendship is leading her to loathe herself. When the two first meet, Doris tells Ruby that she has a pretty face "for a colored girl." After Doris shows Ruby how to make herself look prettier with makeup, Ruby dips her hand in a bucket of white paint and is so pleased with the results that she pours its contents all over her body to conceal her blackness before going to a pep rally with the other students, who ridicule Ruby for her strange appearance.

The Black Hat Man, meanwhile, pushes Lucky further into depression. In the guise of a hardware store proprietor, The Black Hat Man meets Lucky at a display of axes and asks her if she ever thinks "what the brain meat looks like." In this guise, The Black Hat Man is similar to the spectral bartender who pushes Jack Torrance over the edge in the Overlook Hotel. "If some bitch killed my dog," he tells Mrs. Emory, "I might get curious." Later Lucky will have her own "Here's Johnny" moment when, under the influence of The Black Hat Man, she takes a swipe at her daughter Gracie with an axe, because she "needs to save" her daughter in the way that Sethe saved Beloved.

Henry is haunted by demons of his own, which he brought back with him from World War II. He and other Black soldiers were trained to fight, but never allowed to even touch a gun. Instead, Henry's training consisted of his being forced to watch other Black soldiers as they were locked into a chamber full of mustard gas. The sweet smell of this gas makes Henry unable to eat the pie made by his wife and daughters. Henry is also haunted by Da Tap Dance Man (Jeremiah Burkett), a figure in blackface who mocks him while he attempts to fit in with his white coworkers and endure their microaggressions that aren't very micro. Da Tap Dance Man, one of the few Black monsters in *Them,* is a frightening representation of double consciousness, or the internalized conflict experienced by subordinated and/or colonized groups in an oppressive society. Experiencing double consciousness is always looking at one's self through the eyes of a racist white society.

Them is a work of horror in the truest sense of the genre: monsters (a terrifying array of them) do terrible things to good people. *Them* does not pull away from showing scenes that will haunt the viewer's nightmares. We see the family's poor little dog dead and later buried by Henry, who shovels dirt over his companion's bare body without even putting him in a blanket. And we watch the fate of Lucky's infant son while she is gang-raped by the white neighbors in South Carolina who drive the family from their home. And the fantastic elements of *Them* are so terrifying because of how they demonstrate the generational trauma of racism suffered by the Emorys.

The Passion of Guilt: Robert Aickman and *The Good Girl*

Philip Challinor

Among Robert Aickman's selections for the fourth volume in his *Fontana Book of Great Ghost Stories* anthology series was "When I Was Dead," a brief but effective piece by Vincent O'Sullivan (1868–1940). "When I Was Dead" is the narrative of Alistair, a rich young man whose morbid preoccupations have scared all his friends away from his not very cheerful house. Left alone, he tries an occult ritual intended to show "a man or woman who will stay with you during long hours of the night, and may even meet you at unexpected places during the day." The resulting vision is an eyeless crone with black and white hair *à la* Cruella de Vil; just as her eyes begin to appear, Alistair witnesses the servants' discovery of his own dead body, and he subsequently observes, with mounting indignation, the preparations for his funeral. Almost the last image in the story is the "black thread" of the procession winding over a white landscape of snow.

Introducing the story, Aickman commented:

> In all of us the passion of guilt is terrifyingly autonomous: related at once to everything we do and to nothing we have done; strong or weak in us by virtue of forces which have little connection with our actions or conscious thoughts; expressed, more often than not, so indirectly as to build up rather than diminish in the seeming release. . . . "When I Was Dead" is the very rictus or spasm of guilt: sudden and shattering. Vincent O'Sullivan was a master of this dyeing and soaking in guilt. The curious should try to find a copy of his novel, *The Good Girl*. The quest is difficult, but the product distinctive. (*F* 9)

The Internet, which Aickman would doubtless regard with loathing and disdain, has made the quest distinctly less difficult; and being curious, I found a Kindle version. Originally published in 1912, and in a revised edition five years later, *The Good Girl* is neither great nor a ghost story; but it is elegantly written and contains several Aickmanesque adumbrations.

The protagonist is one Paul Vendred, a wealthy young man whose emotional life has been shaped by his Jansenist mother and his various persecutions at a sadistic Catholic school. Vendred conceives a sexual obsession with a singer, Sibyl Dover; and because he lacks the self-confidence simply to pursue her, have her and forget her, he falls in with her family. Her husband lives by talking people out of their money in the name of great schemes and infallible investments, and quickly latches onto Vendred as a promising mark. Eventually Vendred allows himself to be maneuvered into marrying Sibyl's likeable but unsophisticated young stepdaughter, whose lack of social graces proves acutely embarrassing. Too uptight for pleasure and too weak-willed for virtue, Vendred uses the girl as a pretext for seeing her stepmother; but the long-delayed consummation completes his social and financial ruin and drives his wife to despair and death, preceded by the proverbial fate-worse-than. Her father, the confidence trickster, escapes justice because Vendred insists on avoiding scandal at all costs; while the easy-going Mrs. Dover, who has always lacked the self-discipline to pursue the musical career her talent deserves, drapes herself across another rich man's pocket even as her charms definitively fade.

The book came out two years before Aickman's birth, and I have no idea when he first encountered it; but the affinities with his own work are easy to see. The pessimistic, fatalistic plot, with its conclusion in moral and physical decay, must have appealed strongly: "She faded and she changed, as does all that is good," Aickman wrote about an early love of his own (*AR* 62). Even a moralistically dissatisfied *New York Times* review, appended to the Solis Press edition, concedes the quality of the writing; and O'Sullivan, like Aickman, drops in occasional recondite items of vocabulary such as the confidence trickster's "mucedinous" (mildewed) reputation.

Paul Vendred's first name is as Christian as anyone could wish; his surname derives, with tragic irony, from Venus, the Roman goddess of love. Sibyl Dover's first name connotes the pagan oracle, noted for her enigmatic prophecies of inexorable fate; and various minor characters are burdened with surnames like Fippard, Shoulder, and Brodard (embroiderer). Aickman refined this device for his own literary ends with the use of such etymologically loaded names as Lucas Maybury, Clarinda Hartley, Phrynne Banstead, and Nugent Oxenhope. There is also an unsubtle scene of satire against the pretensions of social reformers: a dismal gathering where Vendred encounters "the poet of *Moody Moments*" and "Lambert Mutt, the author of *Recreations of a Tram-conductor,*" and argues about socialism with a middle-aged lady ideologue. This kind of thing could hardly fail to gratify the left-baiting author of "Larger Than Oneself," whose protagonist comes upon "a lesser work by a well-known member of the Labour Party" entitled *Bowel Discipline,* with a jacket illustration realistically depicting "the alimentary system surrounded by a luminous radiation" (*LB* 313).

As to guilt, it is a rather more explicit theme in *The Good Girl* than in "When I Was Dead," not least via some lengthy epigraphs about the fatalistic and pessimistic precepts of Jansenism, which depict humanity as a "poor wreck" tossed by perilous waves, powerless yet unavoidably sinful. Though not conventionally religious, the anti-rationalist Aickman doubtless appreciated the idea of a man driven to disaster by mysterious forces within himself, which his reasoning intellect can observe and analyze but cannot begin to control. The hapless Vendred's buffetings between desire and disappointment must also have been eminently sympathetic to the man who wrote "The Swords," a tale in which the object of obscure male desire is suggestively named Madonna.

The headline of that dissatisfied review, "A Bad Story: Concerning a Good Girl Who Goes Wrong," implies dubiously that the eponymous good girl is Sibyl Dover; while the lady herself, in the novel's last words of dialogue, casually proclaims her late stepdaughter "a good little thing." There is a third candidate: Vendred's self-sanctified, self-martyred mother, whose influence on her son—by virtue of forces that have little connection with her actions or conscious thoughts—predestines him and the rest to their fate.

Works Cited

Aickman, Robert. *The Attempted Rescue.* Horam, UK: Tartarus Press, 2001. [Abbreviated in the text as *AR.*]

———, ed. *The Fourth Fontana Book of Great Ghost Stories.* Glasgow: Fontana, 1967. [Abbreviated in the text as *F.*]

———. *The Late Breakfasters and Other Strange Stories.* Richmond, VA: Valancourt Books, 2016. [Abbreviated in the text as *LB.*]

O'Sullivan, Vincent. *The Good Girl.* Tunbridge Wells, UK: Solis Press, 2013.

To a Puppet, From a Dummy

Jon Padgett

Dolls, mannequins, puppets . . . dummies. First I feared them. Then I pitied them. Then I envied them.

Popular culture presents us with the "killer doll," either as a supernatural hobgoblin or as a psychological delusion born from a ventriloquist's psychotic split personality. As a child, fear of this demon—born of *Night Gallery*'s adaptation of Algernon Blackwood's "The Doll" and, later, "The Dummy" episode from *The Twilight Zone*—possessed and obsessed me. A childlike, uncanny thing moving with non-biological animation was, for me, the height of horror.

Case in point: "The Doll" of *Night Gallery* fame. I saw the episode at the age of four. I had recurring nightmares about the Doll for more than five years following that evening. I can see her even now, forty-five years later, in my imagination. The Doll has a rather square face (like my own) with matted blond hair and smeared black circles under her eyes. When about to kill, the Doll's lids pop open by themselves. Her closed mouth breaks into a fixed grin revealing bright, white teeth. The Doll sits up, opens her eyes, and seems to float toward me.

As per the *Night Gallery* episode plotline, The Doll "lived" only to exact revenge on a predetermined target. She was unstoppable once she had her prey in sight (she could be temporarily destroyed but would always return as good as new to complete her work).

The Doll was more terrifying than any run-of-the-mill horror because of her unchangeable, static glee—baring her teeth and hunting me with a kind of mechanical joy. The Doll never made a sound, and often I couldn't actually see her during my nightmares. But even hidden, I could feel her presence focused like a magnifying glass on my dream self. I might be sneaking in a dreamscape version of my own kitchen and turn to see that a small portrait of a stylized cat was now the hungry visage of the Doll.

I knew she had only to bite me once with her fatal venom to finish the job, as in the television episode, but she seemed content to extend my torment. I felt an unquenchable thirst projected at me by the Doll's unwavering glass eyes and manic, fixed grin. I imagined this empty vessel wanting nothing more than to absorb everything I was or would be into its vacancy. Its clockwork consciousness. Automatonophobia, for me, was simple fear of my identity collapsing and *becoming* that automaton, that *nothing*.

Many nights I would awake screaming after a doll dream, unsure whether I was awake or not. The Doll's small, square face might appear just over the foot of my bed. I can recall countless nights of begging celestial forces to protect me. My prayers were simple: don't let me dream of *her* tonight.

Meanwhile, still a young boy, I began witnessing all too real, waking nightmares: one family dog after another struck and killed by vehicles on the suburban street where we lived. After the first canine death—a beautiful, young sheltie named Sunny—I begged my parents to put up a fence around our house. They refused, but continued taking in dogs. And I witnessed all their violent deaths. In the years that followed, I tried to keep our animals indoors, but at some point I was doomed to slip up.

The last canine death I remember witnessing was that of a female mutt-puppy named Pepper. By then, I was determined not to get close to this dog. I recall the morning my resolve gave way. Pepper stole my heart, as they all did, and I realized I loved her. That same day, she slipped through my legs as I opened the front door to get the mail. It is one of my vivid memories. Pepper slipping out, me yelling her name and running toward her. A car zooming around the far corner down the block. The driver, a teenage boy, seeing Pepper start to toddle across the street. The boy smiling, speeding up, swerving toward Pepper. The impact. My hysterics as the boy pulled over, got out of the car with a snickering friend, and rang our doorbell. My mother opening the door.

"Hey lady, is this your dog?"

"Yes. Would you help me move her body into the backyard?"

"Some people would do that," the boy replies, shrugging, and turns his back on my mother.

The boy and his friend smirk at me and drive off. My sudden fury as I chase after them, screaming, holding the small, broken figure in my hands.

I don't remember how many of these traumatic deaths I witnessed, but I remember the bodies—once energetic and glowing with life, transformed into twitching and, finally, still forms. I see their bright, reflective eyes—so like the Doll's eyes, staring through and beyond me.

And, all the while, the nightly Doll dreams continued. One night the Doll was chasing me as usual through a dream version of my attic. All at once I realized that I was dreaming. Then something unprecedented happened. First, I stopped running and turned on the Doll. Her wicked grin faded into a grimace of doubt. The dream's POV shifted from first to third person. I could now see my own face breaking into the Doll's bloodthirsty, fixed grin. Then I stooped down and grabbed her by one of her tiny, filthy legs, and ripped her limb from limb. To defeat the Doll, I *became* the Doll.

I awoke from my lucid dream, giggling with relief and joy. I thought I was free from my automatonophobia, but soon after I happened to watch the original *Twilight Zone* episode called "The Dummy."

As a child, none of the mannequin-brethren scared me more than ventriloquist dummies. Two things bothered me: first, I didn't know how they could talk by themselves; second, unlike dolls, these figures were large. As I would realize many years later looking at my own three-year-old daughter, ventriloquist dummies are similar in shape and size to human children. They appear alive via the ventriloquist's movements and thrown voice. And when these wooden and plaster child-replicas are "active" in such a way, a willing audience more or less believes in their reality. But it is not the dummy's uncanny movements that are, by themselves, frightening to some of us. It is when the dummy is inert—perhaps sitting on a chair by itself after the show is over—that the real shivers begin. Because we've seen them move and appear to talk on stage, we know those staring, vacant dummy eyes *can* move back and forth. We know that still dummy head *can* swivel. We know that closed dummy mouth *can* open. We know that silent dummy *can* talk. What's more, we now *expect* to see these signs of life even when the ventriloquist is absent. Sit and stare at a dummy in an otherwise empty room, and you'll see what I mean. Sit and stare at the body of a loved one, and you'll feel the same expectancy.

I became a ventriloquist when I was nine years old to stare down this burgeoning dummy fear. I refused to endure more recurring nightmares with a ventriloquist dummy in the Doll's place. That Christmas, I asked my parents for a twenty-five-dollar Mortimer Snerd knockoff. I read the enclosed, three-page pamphlet on the basics of ventriloquism and took to the craft easily. After acclimating to a dummy in my house (and a setback thanks to my cruel and imaginative older brother's shenanigans), my fear abated. I became good at ventriloquism. Then I became excellent at it, performing on stage, booking birthday parties and the like. Three years later, I received a loan from the bank and purchased a custom, professional-grade ventriloquist dummy, which I dubbed Reggie McRascal. He had (and has) real human hair, large blue eyes that wink and blink, a 360-degree swiveling head, and (human hair) eyebrows that move up and down. Aside from darker skin color and a snub nose, in fact, he looks like me.

By that time, my fear of dummies, dolls, and the whole hollow-headed crew had faded away. In fact, I felt a growing affection and pity for my Reggie. I felt guilty when I left him in his case for too long or when I didn't practice with him long enough. He seemed lonely for attention, as if every second in the darkness of the case was a conscious torment for him. When I was a teenager, the dummy and I began having long conversations, which burbled up from my ventriloquist practice sessions. Reggie had become a friend—a more aggressive, funny, angry, and spontaneous version of myself. Fearless—able to say the most awful and hilarious things.

My almost-adult mind knew the dummy was empty, devoid of any kind of consciousness. And yet . . . all those hours staring at myself and him in the mirror imbued Reggie with a kind of phantom personality. I began to imagine I knew what he was thinking. His painted smirk became knowing, sarcastic. Far from wanting to absorb me into an uncanny emptiness, it was as if I had filled *his* hollow form with a kind of unwanted humanity. A human *person*ality. He glowed with it and became ironically larger than life (at least in comparison to my own shy, nascent personality). I expected him to move, to talk, with or even without my unconscious help. This idea was neither uncanny nor monstrous to me. It was normal. One night when I was seventeen, though, a practice session in the mirror became something else. Reggie scolded me at length for my lackluster romantic life. We argued. The dummy made me cry. At some point I realized I had no idea what Reggie was about to say. I cast him down on my bed. Hours had passed since the conversation had begun. I put Reggie back in his case—at the time I thought for good—because I was no longer afraid of the dummy. I was afraid of the human relationship I had formed with what I *knew* was an inanimate object but *felt* was another human being.

College years brought the death of all my grandparents but one, and a big move to another city. I did not take Reggie with me. The years that followed had little to nothing to do with dummies. Reggie became a bizarre footnote in my life, an oddity to pull out for friends and family on rare occasions when the spirit moved me. Of course, I was careful to put him away shortly after taking him out, lest Reggie began speaking again of his own accord.

In the meantime, my attitude toward all automata changed. Long gone were the days when a creepy, big-eyed, staring doll could keep me from sitting alone in a room with it. On the contrary, I started to develop a deep feeling of connection to and affection for my little hollow friends. I couldn't have said why at the time.

I had my first bout of significant depression as a young adult. With college done, it was as if the future ahead had folded into itself. I had long known that extinction was the destiny of all living things, but now I *felt* that black hole of mortality pulling me toward it. I moved into a small apartment and brought Reggie with me, now out of his case, sitting on a chair in my tiny living room. I never practiced with the dummy—too despondent to attempt such a thing—but I could no longer bear to leave him locked up in a suitcase. I identified with him and his mannequin-brethren more than ever. Like them, I was subject to forces beyond my control, helpless in an unknowable universe.

I swung back and forth between the poles of despair and panic in nauseating, wide arcs. I recall the utter stillness of the apartment each late night as I tried to sleep, plagued with an unwanted flood of compulsive thoughts. Soon after moving in, I started hearing a steady clacking from the living room outside the open bedroom door. It was the unmistakable hollow sound of a dummy's plaster mouth opening and snapping shut in the darkness. I remember fearing he was moving out there by himself. I remember hoping he was.

As the days turned to weeks and months, my world began emptying out. I left the apartment only to fetch junk food and work, which I did with automatic tedium. My coworkers had become puppets, pulled this way and that by supervisors or their own senseless compulsions. This perspective was not limited to others. Every time I looked in a mirror, I saw a panicked, wide-eyed dummy staring back at me.

Meanwhile, I had long ago stopped cleaning up after myself. Dishes were piled high and molding, never to be washed again. Trash was rarely taken out and accumulated in grocery bags in the kitchen and living room. Soda bottles littered the filthy wall-to-wall carpeting. The bathtub looked and smelled like a swamp. Soon the whole apartment resembled one. The apartment attracted a terrible ant infestation, which I allowed to prosper—sometimes spending late afternoons after work watching lines of the tiny automata marching along, following orders from compulsions they could neither control nor understand.

Every night I heard what I imagined was Reggie's mouth clacking in the living room. Open pause pause clack. Open pause pause clack. And now, night or day, whenever I closed my eyes, I envisioned rapid-fire images of self-violence. A bullet exploding out of my skull, spewing brain matter on the apartment wall. A steak knife plunging into my stomach, ruined intestines and bloody shit squirming out of me. Fingernails wrenched off one by one with needle-nose pliers. Understand: I didn't *want* to do harm to myself—let alone kill myself. These terrifying images were my new waking nightmares.

Now when I looked in the mirror, I saw a dummy in an aspect of despair and terror. But I saw a glint of something more—the staring eyes of my long-lost dogs, Sunny and Pepper and the rest, staring through and beyond me.

I spent a lot of time sitting in the living room when I returned from my work at the library, staring at Reggie's inert form. The sight of a motionless ventriloquist dummy may drive people insane if they stare at it long enough, just as staring too long at a corpse might. We are afraid (hope) that both dummy and corpse will move again. And this fear (desire) might make us wonder whether our *own* animation (both physical and mental) is as artificial as the dummy's.

I stopped paying all my bills. The power company and credit card collection services inundated me with angry letters and phone calls. Then my phone was disconnected.

One evening, soon after discovering an eviction notice on my door, I tried to move the dummy's eyes with my mind. I sat across from him in the semi-darkness, and—after at least an hour of mesmerized staring—Reggie's eyes shifted to the left. I screamed and fell and got up, stumbling backwards into my filmy living-room glass door and out of it onto my tiny balcony. Hyperventilating. Afraid to enter the black rectangle of the door. Afraid of what I had done to Reggie. Afraid of what I had done to my own mind.

I sought and received help via psychiatric drugs and psychotherapy shortly thereafter. Depression and panic and delusions subsided with time. I moved, of course (sans security deposit and with a nasty stain on my credit record). But my year alone with Reggie in that terrible, quiet, disgusting apartment changed me and my relationship to the dummy and its mannequin-brethren. My fascination with these figures never abated, but my complicated fear and naïve pity of them morphed into nostalgia and empathy. I now felt a kinship with them.

Following my mental breakdown, I spent the better part of the next twenty years working out a simple question. What it is about dolls, dummies, puppets, and mannequins that unnerves and fascinates?

What I have discovered is this: these anthropomorphic, hollow-headed bugaboos are too much like us, both alive and dead. Some years ago I was diagnosed with a cerebral aneurysm. It unmoored me from my "life's story" and forced me to stare down into the impossible blankness beyond consciousness. Aren't we all terrified and fascinated to one degree or another by our *own* inevitable dummyhood? Isn't that both the struggle and paradox of our collective existence as sentient organisms? We eventually will be just as inert—just as empty—as they are.

But, unlike us, our mannequin-brethren never suffer. There is no middle ground of consciousness between poles of empty forever. Consider the dummy, sans ventriloquist, sitting there by itself in an ideal state of meditative emptiness—neither alive nor dead. The dummy is a trifle. It is and always has been nothing.

And this brings me to the feeling I have now whenever I pull the dummy out of its case.

I envy the dummy. I admire it.

Why? It has not aged. All that time in its case, all those years, have meant protection from the elements, from time itself. Any flaw—a bit of rubbed-off paint on the neck from plastic neck hole friction, for instance—can be mended. Not even dust has been allowed to collect on the dummy. Next to any biological organism, it is ageless. As humans, we are not so lucky. The skeleton-dummies inside us wear down and become brittle with the years. The joints become painful and worn until they are unusable. The skin that covers them becomes sagging, wrinkled, and papery thin—quick to tear. Our movement slows until we are inert things. Our brains shrink and malfunction. Our hearts tire and sicken. This degeneration is inherent to our being. Is it any wonder that our ancestors worshipped idols, which have a semi-permanence our own bodies and minds lack?

And that leads me back to where I started all those years ago as a child running away from the Doll in the endless hallways of my nightmares. I haven't had a dream about her since I was nine years old. But if—as the elderly man I may become—I could turn around upon the Doll, I wouldn't set a toothy grin upon my face and rip her limb from limb, as I once did. No. I would surrender to her. I would sit down, draw her into my arms, and let the greedy void inside that tiny body consume anything left of my human identity. My life story.

Yes, I envy the Doll and her mannequin-brethren. They look like us, yet they are more serene than we can ever hope to be. As living beings, I used to imagine that Reggie had a *personality*. I realize now that it was all me—the illness that is my own consciousness, my perceived separateness from the inanimate past and future projected into a hollow piece of wood, plaster, and paint made to resemble a human being. *I* am the one still possessed with the unrelenting idea that I am a person. But Reggie has never shared this ailment. *I*—not the dummy—am the one who fights back the rapid-fire, compulsive memories and future-projections that ricochet through my mind every waking moment of the day.

The dummy is the answer. The dummy is my future.

The dummy is *your* future.

When I take Reggie out of its dusty old case these days and perform, usually for my daughter or an audience of one in the mirror, the dummy's manner couldn't be more different from what it was those many years ago. The dummy is physically unchanged, but the words I throw into it have become shy, childlike, kind, nascent. It is never aggressive nor angry.

When I look at it, I know the dummy sees me, though—the real me.

I recognize myself in the bright, reflecting nothingness of its eyes.

"To a Puppet, From a Dummy" was first published in *Mannequin: Tales of Wood Made Flesh,* ed. Justin Burnett (Silent Motorist Media, 2019).

The Horror of the American Body

Javier Martinez

JEFFREY THOMAS. *The American*. Carbondale, IL: Journal-Stone Publishing, 2020. 266 pp. $17.95 tpb. ISBN: 9781950305414.

Beginning with his short stories first published in the early 1990s, Jeffrey Thomas has become a prolific and versatile writer. From his Punktown series of novels and stories, to his Hades sequence, to the many other story landscapes he plays in, Thomas has steadily carved out a narrative niche that is very much his own. Thomas effortlessly, and lovingly, embraces genre: body horror, supernatural horror, Lovecraft-inspired horror and pastiche, science fiction world-building, crime, and even travel narrative of sorts (inspired by his love of Vietnam and Vietnamese culture). His latest novel, *The American,* is perhaps his most focused work, deeply immersed in contemporary Vietnam; it is also his least overtly fantastic work (in John Clute's use of the term), eschewing for the most part supernatural or science fictional elements for a psychic insight or vision that is the manifestation of the main character's PTSD. This is not to say, however, that *The American* is a tame novel that might serve to ease the wary reader into Thomas's oeuvre. *The American* tells a deeply disturbing and even tragic story, and it is relentless in its exhibition and exposition of the deformed and disfigured body. Given such a focus, it would be easy for Thomas to turn his characters into a sideshow attraction and his novel into a hack piece that flounders due to its exploitive superficiality. Instead, he manages to maintain a dignity to his narrative and his characters (as debased as some of them may be) that will satisfy self-styled literary aficionados and hardcore readers alike.

The plot of *The American* is straightforward enough. Richard Trenor, a disfigured Vietnam veteran, is contacted by Tanh, the son of Trenor's Vietnamese partner-in-arms Quan, when his sisters go missing. Trenor flies to Vietnam, reunites with his old friend, and helps Tanh search for his missing family. Along the way they cross paths with an American hitman of Vietnamese descent and a serial pedophile and killer referred to as Bedford, after the protagonist of H. G. Wells's *The First Men in the Moon*. The otherwise action-film plot is problematized by a cast of characters nearly all of whom have some physical abnormality or emotional issue. Tanh, for example, suffers from Ectrodactyly and is referred to as Mr. Crab, and his father Quan, a widower, has descended into alcoholism and self-loathing. As the story develops the reader comes to understand the unique consequence or side effect of Trenor's military experience. After recovering from a gunshot to the face, Trenor is able to "see" a person's moral failings, which manifest themselves as small spider-like creatures that scuttle in and out of people's skin and openings. The more crawlies Trenor sees, the more debased the person. The various plotlines in the story dovetail eventually, with every chapter and section of the novel gradually magnifying, but never glorifying, the level of violence. While there is not much of a mystery to uncover, the gradual working out of the characters' traumas makes for an engaging if sometimes unsettling read. By the end of the book, Thomas has deftly woven all the narrative threads together into a cohesive story. Aside from some questions about Bedford's character, which I discuss below, the story manages to be both satisfying and disturbing.

The eponymous American of the title refers specifically to the unnamed and elegant, if icy, hitman who carries out his trade under the guise of a curio importer. Born in Vietnam, "he had been raised in the United States since arriving as one of the 'boat people' at the age of ten" and now, "at forty-two, he appeared young and healthy, had smooth, agreeable features, his black hair neatly cut and silky with gel, his customary white linen suit perfectly tailored." But the title could just as well refer to the novel's main character Richard Trenor, a Vietnam War veteran burdened by his physical and psychological trauma:

> He was still trim for a man of sixty. For years following his return to the States he had worn his hair long and unruly, along with a scruffy beard as if to curtain and cover his scars, but over the years the beard had diminished to his current neatly groomed mustache and goatee and his hair had returned to a bristling short military look, albeit these days glinting throughout with silver. . . . Those scars of his not masked by the eye patch included a pale seam down the center of his forehead, where the edges of skin had been sewn together after a flap had been lifted there and rotated down to reconstruct the smashed bridge of his nose . . . which remained misshapen, looking stitched together from differently hued patches of skin. Other faded but still noticeable scars traced their way around this right cheek.

Or the American could be Bedford the serial killer, whom Trenor initially meets psychically in his dreams and in person late in the novel, after he has been reduced to a beggar disfigured by his own hand: "The man couldn't enunciate his words well because he had no lips, just a skull's bared yellow teeth in a raw mask of scar tissue. No nose . . . just slits in its place. Only holes where ears had been. No hair, as if he had not only been shaved but scalped. He looked like an anatomical model, a cadaver who had healed the best he could after partial dissection." This sad triptych—the clinical assassin, the soulful hero, and the monster (not because of his looks, but because of his actions)—while very different from one another, nevertheless share a common feature: they are the result of exposure to some external force larger than themselves. For the killer, it is his childhood experiences as a refugee. For Trenor, it is the scars he carries and the psychic ability he has gained from his experience in the war. And for Bedford, it is a madness that descends upon him once he has left the sheltering environment of his country and home.

In Thomas's universe, to be an American is to be twisted, broken, and maimed—a tragic trio of traits, to be sure; and, even worse, to be an American is to export those qualities onto a world stage where everyone and everything is affected. Thomas is not so naive as to think that the U.S. is the sole exporter of debauchery and violence. The novel is full of instances of transgressions against the moral order on an international scale. Take, for instance, the sad case of Lucky, a female orangutan forced into a life of prostitution in Indonesia. Actual humans do not fare any better: Tanh's sister Tra Mi's works as a bar girl and Bedford's partner, Hong, is a woman "whose entire face was profoundly disfigured with scar tissue, giving the appearance of a crude latex Halloween mask. She might have been mistaken for the victim of an acid attack, but Trenor guessed it was most likely the result of napalm."

Thomas walks a fine line here. Experienced readers may not flinch too much at such scenes, especially those familiar with the extreme horror found at the margins of the genre. But as I note in the opening paragraph, Thomas avoids turning *The American* into a grindhouse feature by imbuing his characters, even his most corrupted, with a certain dignity. The assassin, like all anti-heroes, adheres to a code of behavior from which he refuses to deviate. Trenor is at heart a good man, lonely and burdened by his past and by the moment he now finds himself in.

But it is Bedford who is most fascinating because of the contradictions in his character and in the contradictory ways in which the novel presents him. Trenor never sees Bedford's real face, only his psychic one: "The beggar had no face. His entire head was nothing but a seething ball of black spider-things, so thick upon him they buried his features—substituted for his features." Readers witness Bedford's descent from traveling businessman to deranged predator, but we also see his moment of psychic insight into his nature, a self-knowledge that leads him literally to flay himself in an attempt to exorcise his pedophilic bloodlust. He succeeds, but at the cost of self-mutilation. Trenor's view of Bedford clearly implies Bedford's ongoing depraved moral state, but this characterization seems undercut just a few pages later when we are told that Bedford is careful not to let Hong's grand-niece get too close to him: "Sometimes the youngest girl, a pretty little thing named Trinh, having known him all her life, would climb into his lap, but it made Bedford uneasy and he'd gently lift her away. If she sat upon him too long, he'd begin feeling tickles of itchiness in his scars. He hadn't felt profoundly itchy since the night of transformation. He didn't want to feel that way again." Bedford makes a conscious decision to control and tamp down his desires, and while he has never paid for his actions in a legal sense, he has nevertheless attempted to make amends through his self-mortification and through his commitment to Hong and her extended family. In other words, he is conscious of his past and he wants to make something better of his future, even if it is only as a beggar on the streets of Vietnam.

More than Trenor or the unnamed American, both of whom remain stubbornly in character throughout the novel, Bedford is the one character who experiences profound emotional, psychological, and physical change. That arc of development can be difficult to trace: at what point in the story is Bedford a fully realized character with a complexity that defies any easy categorization? It cannot be when we first meet him, as a generic "lost American" making his way through the streets of Vietnam. It is not when he is on his raping and killing spree. It is not even immediately after his transformation, an awful scene that details his self-inflicted punishment. It is perhaps at the end of the novel when Thomas makes the reader feel something for this evil, sad, tragic, pitiful man (and, by extension, Hong as well). Thomas manages a deft narrative move here, especially given that Bedford's story arc plays so well off of Thanh's, whose development, while not as extreme or graphic, is nevertheless chilling in its own way, if only because his decision at the end of the book is understandable. I do not want to give too much away about the book's plot, even though most readers will likely anticipate what is coming.

The American may lack some of the pure imaginative force of Thomas's other work, especially the Punktown stories and his more science-fiction-flavored novels; but *The American* may be his most focused and sustained work to date, which is high praise for a writer who consistently produces quality work that substantively contributes to the fields of horror, science fiction, and fantasy. It is probably too extreme to succeed as a crossover novel that will gain him a wider audience, but *The American,* and Thomas's work in general, deserves that audience nonetheless.

The Many Lives of Mina Murray

Karen Joan Kohoutek

Since its publication in 1897, Bram Stoker's *Dracula* has been adapted at a steady rate to new forms of media. In most of these new versions, the character of Jonathan Harker, the lawyer who meets the vampire in Transylvania, is a fixed point, as are occult expert Dr. Van Helsing and Renfield, who becomes Dracula's minion. Small details may change, and occasionally larger tweaks to the storyline occur, but if these men appear, their names, basic characteristics, and roles within the storyline almost invariably remain the same.

The situation of Mina Murray is very different. She begins the story as Jonathan's fiancée, marries him to become Mina Harker, and becomes the final victim of Dracula's thirst, whom the other characters rally to save from becoming a vampire herself. Through the long history of Dracula adaptations, there is a noticeable tendency to change her storyline and essential personality dramatically, especially compared to the male characters, who remain much more consistent. In some adaptations, her role is minimized to near erasure, and the character is frequently interchanged with her friend Lucy Westenra, with their names and aspects of each other's storylines swapped around.

Lucy, who precedes her as Dracula's victim, plays a significant part in Stoker's book, but she is killed midway through, making her more of a secondary character. Lucy's three suitors from the novel are also frequently shuffled around in adaptations, with some changed drastically (for example, the 1927 play changes Dr. Seward from Lucy's love interest to Mina's father, which carries into later versions) or removed completely. These are all secondary characters in the novel (compared to the Harkers and Van Helsing) and, in being intimately connected to Lucy, reflect her malleability. As Lucy's role changes, their roles inevitably change with it.

Mina, however, is one of the central characters in Stoker's

book; arguably the most important, after Van Helsing and Dracula himself. This raises the question of why she has been considered so mutable, and why new creators feel so free to change the details of her background and her essential personality into whatever their plots or their fancy require.

In particular, most of the adaptations veer away from the active, sensible Mina Murray of Stoker's novel. In the 1922 film *Nosferatu,* she is turned into a self-sacrificing wife who doesn't survive the adaptation; in the iconic 1931 *Dracula,* starring Bela Lugosi, she is a damsel in distress with limited screen time; in John Badham's 1979 *Dracula,* she's a romantic and eventually transgressive woman; in *Bram Stoker's Dracula* (1992), she is passionately committed to her love for Dracula. By the 2014 Showtime series *Penny Dreadful,* the pragmatic Mina Harker and her prosaic lawyer husband have no place within the program's R-rated melodrama, and from their one-time position as primary protagonists they are entirely sidelined.

Although the names and identities of other characters are occasionally shifted, it most consistently occurs with Mina, over multiple adaptations, even when the change does nothing to streamline the plot. There are obviously too many versions of *Dracula* to deal with them all in depth, but I have tried to cover several of the more well-known adaptations, along with the long-running and influential play, the source for the 1931 and 1979 films, starring Bela Lugosi and Frank Langella, retrospectively. First produced in 1924 and revised in 1927, the play's popularity substantially increased Dracula's name recognition, and several of its revisions stuck in the popular imagination; perhaps aided by Lugosi's casting.

Dracula, by Bram Stoker (1897)

In the original novel, Mina Murray is an orphaned schoolteacher, the fiancée of Jonathan Harker, a middle-class working lawyer whom she marries during the book. She has some access to a more elite social circle, having been quasi-adopted by the wealthy family of Lucy Westenra, an old school friend. Lucy is a charismatic flirt and a foil for Mina, who is consistently depicted as an eminently sensible woman who has long been supporting herself with her own job.

Adaptations have tended to place her in an elevated social class, giving her a lifestyle and social status similar to that of Lucy in the novel. Even the versions, like that in 1992, that mention her role as adopted friend, out of her sphere, continue to show her in wealthy settings, wearing expensive-looking gowns.

Mina's introduction in the novel creates a very different impression, and its details already help define the character she will display throughout:

> I have been simply overwhelmed with work. The life of an assistant schoolmistress is sometimes trying . . . I have been working very hard lately, because I want to keep up with Jonathan's studies, and I have been practising shorthand very assiduously. When we are married I shall be able to be useful to Jonathan, and if I can stenograph well enough I can take down what he wants to say in this way and write it out for him on the typewriter, at which also I am practising very hard. (53)

She later refers to their married life beginning in a "simple way," in which they will need to "make both ends meet" (74). She describes them as "people of our modest bringing up" (157) who need to work for a living, and her background as an orphan is made clear: "I never knew either father or mother" (157). When Harker's employer dies, the young couple inherits his house, and this is a major windfall to them (154). Characteristically, Mina is concerned that this has made her "rusty in my shorthand—see what unexpected prosperity does for us" (171).

The very ordinariness of Jonathan and Mina is a part of the original novel's texture, setting the supernatural against a backdrop of everyday life. It is possible that this mundane focus on middle-class life doesn't seem "Victorian" enough to a modern audience, who expects certain style cues and ambience in what is considered "Victorian."

Mina, whose love and loyalty for Jonathan are never in question during the novel, is seen in contrast to Lucy, who vacillates between her suitors. Mina and Jonathan have planned a working partnership, and that is how they embark on their married life. There may be some echo here of Stoker's relationship with his wife, Florence Balcombe, in the picture of the Harkers' marriage. In his later life, facing serious illness, Stoker wrote his brother that his wife was "an angel . . . She had to do all the bookkeeping and find the money to live on—God only knows how she managed" (Belford 279).

In contrast, it is treated as a coincidence that Lucy just happens to choose the suitor with a title and a fortune, as if that isn't part of her reasoning, but it is hard not to notice that he is the most eligible in worldly terms.

Mina's real value to the novel comes to the foreground when she reads her husband's journal from his Transylvanian experience, and her immediate reaction is to type it up as a record. She has already typed up her own journals, detailing her visit with Lucy and her friend's illness, and these provide invaluable evidence for Van Helsing.

The men begin trying to protect her, but she tells them, "I have not faltered" (221), showing courage and fortitude. While the novel is grounded in Christian belief, Mina's strongest faith is in information. She cross-references all their evidence and builds a chronological timetable of events (222–24). Her process is very efficient, using mimeograph paper to type multiple copies at once and collating everything, including newspaper accounts (225). This includes transcribing all Dr. Seward's notes, which he recited into an early Dictaphone.

Despite her key part in the investigation, the men are still paternalistic toward her. Van Helsing insists she be shut out at times, because the "a risk [is] so great." He even gives her a sedative, making her more vulnerable to attack (286). Once she has been bitten by the vampire and her psychic link with Dracula is established, for a time they do need to keep things from her, so their enemy won't know their plans. Eventually, though, it is Mina who compiles all the elements of the problem, breaking it down and formulating the plan they will follow to destroy him (350–53).

When Dracula flees to Transylvania, she even knows offhand that the train they need to catch will leave "at 6:30 tomorrow morning!" The men are amazed at her knowledge, but she has been keeping an eye on the railroad time-tables, and "I knew that if anything were to take us to Castle Dracula we should go by Galatz, or at any rate through Bucharest . . .Unhappily there are not many to learn, as the only train tomorrow leaves as I say" (338).

Although it is not often remarked upon, the novel itself begins with a preface explaining that "how these papers have been placed in sequence will be made clear in the reading of them" (xxviii). The novel itself shows Mina as the fictional editor who collected them into the text, with her husband's help, from the "exactly contemporary" accounts she originally transcribed.

Nosferatu: A Symphony of Horror (1922)

While following the general outline of *Dracula,* this German-language silent film, "freely composed" from the novel, according to the opening credits, is truncated and transferred to a German village. These larger-scale changes, which include removing Lucy and her suitors completely, reflect less on the specifics of Mina and Jonathan, renamed Ellen and Hutter, but are still of some interest.

The Mina character, Ellen, is strongly associated with domesticity, with scenes of her performing household tasks, like sewing. Her life seems to revolve completely around her husband: when he plans to leave for his business trip to the vampire's castle, she is immediately distressed and dresses as if in mourning to see him off, in a black veil and gown. She seems to have a premonition of what is to come and has almost a psychic bond with her husband, waking up in the night when he is on his way back, crying, "I have to go to him, he is coming!"

Ellen becomes active and heroic, but enacts this by sacrificing herself. She destroys the vampire by luring him in to attack her, distracting him until sunrise. In doing so, she saves the whole town, stopping the manifestation of the plague he brought with him. This can only be done by a maiden who is giving her blood willingly, so her willingness for self-sacrifice becomes her defining feature.

A 1979 remake, *Nosferatu, the Vampyre,* sticks fairly closely to this storyline, in an expanded version. It does restore the names of the characters, so Hutter turns back to Jonathan Harker, but it follows the lead of the later play in renaming his wife Lucy Harker.

Dracula, by Hamilton Deane (1924) and Hamilton Deane & John L. Balderston (1927)

The first iteration of the *Dracula* theatrical production, from 1924, follows the relationships of the novel fairly closely, beginning with a married Jonathan and Mina Harker, with Lucy as a friend who died prior to the play. Its major innovation lies in changing Dracula to a neighbor and getting him directly involved with the other characters' lives. In the novel, Dracula isn't seen by anyone, apart from Harker's visit to Transylvania, until page 172; but here, Harker has sold the property to Dracula as a straightforward transaction, without any Transylvanian drama, and the cast has gotten to know him without suspicion. Also, Quincy Morris has become a pistol-packing woman, but that change didn't stick in later versions.

Lucy's illness has the familiar trajectory, but she has died before the start of the play, which begins with the already married Mina Harker suffering some of the same symptoms. In both versions of the play, and the 1931 film, the details of Lucy's illness in the novel are transferred to Mina's experience: the bad dreams, the garlic in her room, and so on.

The 1927 revision makes several significant adaptations, switching the names and rearranging family connections. Mina is renamed Lucy Seward, the daughter of Dr. Seward, but is engaged to Harker; her friend, renamed Mina, still died prior to the play. These names will transfer to the 1979 version, based on a Broadway revival of this play, but with some changes, keeping both women alive in the beginning so their storyline is in line with the Stoker original.

By being turned into Dr. Seward's daughter, Mina loses her original status as an orphan and a woman earning her own living. From this point, the majority of adaptations will put her in a family with other characters, usually one wealthier than where she began.

In both the 1924 and 1927 versions, Mina/Lucy is so horrified by what is happening to her that she longs for death, explicitly considering suicide, to which Van Helsing vehemently objects. This concern for her immortal soul is straight out of Stoker, but is largely removed from later adaptations, which are more secular, despite the frequent crucifixes. Only *Penny Dreadful,* in which a character wrestles with her intense Catholic faith, contains any real echoes of this theme.

As with the novel, the texts of neither play contain any hint whatsoever that Mina/Lucy was ever attracted to Dracula. It may be that the charisma of the actors, including Bela Lugosi, originally added this element to the lore. It may also be that the very act of depicting, in an embodied way, what could be more ambiguous on the page was an influence; that is, visibly seeing the woman succumb to his embrace might bring out a subtext that was originally submerged. Either way, in these early versions Dracula appears as a true predator, most akin to a version of the villain Killgrave from *Jessica Jones,* who uses his mental powers to steal the will and freedom of women to manipulate and sexually abuse them, which is rightly treated as a horrific violation.

Dracula (1931)

This film version of Deane and Balderston's play, with its stage star Bela Lugosi in the lead, is a major milestone in *Dracula*'s enduring popularity, but it is undeniable that the roles of the female characters are greatly reduced. This is particularly noticeable when one comes to the film version directly from Stoker's novel, without having seen the play.

It follows the play fairly closely, although it changes Mina and Lucy's first names back to the original versions. Mina remains Dr. Seward's daughter, however; Jonathan Harker's first name is shortened to John, and Lucy is included in living form, to meet and become attracted to Dracula, saying "He's fascinating." Mina retorts, "Give me someone a little more normal," and Lucy teases her, "Like John?" This interaction evokes more of their relationship in the novel than is sometimes seen.

The restoration of Mina and Lucy's original names may relate to the addition of the lawyer's visit to Transylvania, which is transferred from the novel (albeit changing the character to Renfield), but doesn't appear in the theatrical versions. The basic storyline of the play is fused into a hybrid with elements from Stoker's original, bringing in the visually dramatic scenes in Dracula's castle, but maintaining a plot that allows Lugosi to interact with the rest of the cast in a way he couldn't do if it were more faithful.

Oddly, Lucy's death is almost skipped over. One minute Dracula is leaning over here, and the next she is on the autopsy table. If you miss one line of dialogue, you wouldn't know what happened to her. From then on, Mina becomes largely a damsel in distress, suffering from the kind of vampire persecution Lucy did in the novel, rather than taking an active role.

Horror of Dracula (1958)

The characters in this film, famous as Christopher Lee's debut in the role of Dracula, are rearranged here in a new and distinctive way. The two canonically engaged couples swap partners, seemingly arbitrarily, so that Jonathan Harker is engaged to Lucy Holmwood, the sister of Arthur Holmwood (rather than his fiancée). He in turn is married to Mina Holmwood. Despite the partner switch, Lucy and Mina have roughly the same identities and storylines they have in the novel.

In this version, Arthur is very much a stuffed shirt. In her first scene, Mina barely moves, and looks imprisoned by her stiff, enormous gown. Lucy, introduced in bed, is sickly and already under Dracula's power. She looks very youthful, with a soft, young-sounding voice, and unlike the flirtatious Lucy, the combined effect makes her appear particularly innocent and childlike. As soon as she is alone, however, she jumps up, full of energy, to open her window for Dracula, and then sprawls on the bed to wait for him.

Director Terence Fisher, by various accounts, seems to have prided himself on bringing the novel's undertones of repressed sexuality to the surface and forefront of Dracula lore, although in the novel this is arguably more prominent in Lucy's storyline, as well as Jonathan's encounters with the women at Dracula's castle, than in Mina's. After Lucy's death, Mina is lured to Dracula under the belief that she is meeting her husband, but there are strong visual cues expressing a sexual attraction. When she comes the next morning, she looks happy and self-satisfied, even a little smug. In the end she is saved, and she embraces her overbearing husband in a happy ending, but before Dracula threw her into an open grave she appeared to be enjoying a secret adultery with him more than suffering from unwanted contact.

Count Dracula (1977)

This BBC television production remains one of the most faithful adaptations, but there are still distinctive changes. Mina is engaged to Jonathan Harker, and she and Lucy are sisters, with the last name Westenra. They share the original Lucy's social status, with Mina wearing long frothy gowns and elaborate hats that mark her as wealthy. Still the more sensible of the two, Mina mentions her study of shorthand, which is an appreciated detail. Here Lucy is being courted by Dr. Seward and Quincy Holmwood, a hybrid of her other two suitors.

Lucy is lively and sprightly, where Mina is afraid of both the storm and the old man at the graveyard, which makes her seem more sensitive, a little fragile even, in comparison. True to the novel, a thread runs throughout that shows the men keeping the women ignorant, which puts them in danger. Both Lucy's continued exposure (due to their not explaining the reason for the garlic in her room) and the initial attack on Mina (who has been left alone, supposedly to protect her) could have been prevented had the men trusted the women and shared information with them.

Mina does exhibit some nerve when she goes to see Renfield at the asylum, and eventually takes some charge of the situation so that, as in the novel, Van Helsing comments upon her wisdom, although her reduced role makes this somewhat less motivated and more out of the blue.

Dracula (1979)

Based on the1927 play, with Frank Langella, star of its recent Broadway revival, as the Count, this film switches the female characters back again to their names in the play. The Mina character is Lucy, Dr. Seward's daughter, and, in a new twist, her friend Mina is the daughter of Dr. Van Helsing. All the characters seem to be laced together in strange connections: while Jonathan still sold the house to Dracula without incident, as in the play, now the house used to belong to Renfield, who is resentful about it.

This Lucy is confident and outgoing, although she maintains an air of gravity and poise, even respectability, an echo of the character in the novel. She is engaged to Jonathan Harker, but it seems more like an informal understanding, with no sense of urgency. Her potential ambivalence about settling down possibly frees her to pursue her attraction to Dracula, which makes infidelity less of an issue. Even before that, she is shown to have independent interests, reading a letter out loud about how she will "make a beautiful addition" to a firm "as soon as you finish law school." This is definitely an expansion from her shorthand studies and desire to be an assistant to Jonathan in his law practice, although it doesn't receive any more development than this.

This Mina, on the other hand, is not the vibrant flirt that so many versions of Lucy remain at their cores. She is a relatively fragile, physically weak young woman, whom Lucy is "looking after" during an ongoing illness that predated Dracula's arrival. She is strong enough to leave the house and wander outside, but is easily susceptible to his influence.

Once introduced to their social circle, Dracula is openly seductive to both women, arousing Jonathan's jealousy, which is not misplaced. Before long, his supposed fiancée is sneaking off for unchaperoned visits with their handsome neighbor, and, by the time they hunt him down in the end, she seems to be genuinely in love with him. This seems like an earlier draft of the relationship in the upcoming *Bram Stoker's Dracula,* in which the Mina character clearly prefers a generations-old love for Dracula to a middle-class marriage with Jonathan.

Bram Stoker's Dracula (1992)

In this very successful film adaptation, Mina Harker and Lucy are more or less restored to their positions, but, in a story that revels in the impulse to make the villain romantic, Mina becomes the reincarnation of Dracula's long-dead true love. In an opening flashback, Winona Ryder, the actress who plays Mina, is seen as Dracula's wife, who commits suicide when she thinks the historical warrior prince has been killed. This dramatic past-life love story colors the perception of the present-day Mina, who seems to be the reincarnation of this noblewoman.

Much was made at the time of this version's faithfulness to Stoker's novel, although in many ways it is less so than almost any previous adaptation. However, it is striking to note that, of all the versions discussed so far, this is the first to restore Mina to her original last name, Murray, since the 1897 novel. In the first version of the play, she was already married and turned into Mina Harker by marriage.

The tendency to elevate her to a higher social status is still on display, since she is seen sitting in a palatial garden and is always elegantly dressed. She is also outgoing and physically demonstrative, in contrast to the novel's Mina, who worried it was "very improper" to walk arm in arm with her husband (171), blaming it on her "years teaching etiquette and decorum." That sort of comment can, of course, be used as evidence of sexual repression, but that is a supposition, not a fact. Her cognizance that others will judge the propriety of public behavior isn't proof of either her inward feelings or her private behavior with Jonathan, both of which were necessarily veiled from view due to the publication standards of the time.

Like *Horror of Dracula,* themes of sexuality are presented more overtly. Lucy, for example, is more than flirty, and constantly making double entendres; Mina insists on her being moral and virtuous underneath it all, but it is not all clear that this view is correct.

Unusually, the class issue is acknowledged in this film. Mina, staying with the wealthy Westenras, mentions being "only a schoolmistress," as in the novel, but now Jonathan, a poor lawyer, feels inferior to her rich friends, which this film expands into a conflict between them.

In this version, Dracula pursues Mina after seeing her picture, recognizing her as a vision of his long-dead wife, and possibly her reincarnation. Given that, it is not clear why he first attacks Lucy. It is strange that of all the women in London he might have fed from in the short term, he decides to seduce his true love's best friend. While Lucy's barely repressed sexuality may make her susceptible to his seductive energy, this subplot makes more sense in the other versions, where Mina wasn't an original, specific object of desire.

Eventually they have a conversation about this, in which, upset, she rightfully states, "You murdered Lucy," but almost immediately declares, "I want to be what you are . . . You are my love, and my life."

During the time when Jonathan is missing, Mina pursues a relationship with Dracula, aware of her developing feelings for him, but then marries Jonathan, thinking he must never know about her "Sweet Prince." The emphasis on his being a prince seems relevant, given that Jonathan, the "poor lawyer," was worried that her head would be turned by her proximity to wealth, a detail that only exists in this version. Like the original Lucy marrying the most wealthy and highly placed of her suitors, this doesn't seem like a coincidence, especially since this schoolteacher is really royalty reincarnated.

Throughout their courtship period, and after, it is unclear how much we are meant to assume that Dracula is hypnotizing Mina, since she does at times seem to be in a trance. Is she remembering her past life or just flirting crazily with a stranger instead of looking for her fiancé? Even as she seems to respond freely to Dracula, in a kind of sexual awakening, she still seems to lack agency.

In the book, Mina was put into a hypnotic state, her free will and ability to resist totally removed, which, while terrible, clarified that she wasn't complicit in what was happening to her. The character in *Bram Stoker's Dracula* seems more lacking in agency, since some of their scenes suggest hypnotism, but Mina also, seemingly of her own volition, abandons her loyalties to Lucy and Jonathan, and insists on Dracula turning her into one of the undead.

The film's tag line, prominent on the poster and other advertising, was "Love Never Dies," with an image of the two embracing. This supports an interpretation that this is intended as a love story, in which the two find each other again after centuries apart, ignoring the brutality of Dracula's behavior and robbing Mina of any moral response to it. She is far from the character who thought suicide would be preferably to becoming a vampire, with all it entailed.

While this version restores her proper name and occupation, and general social status, and relationships to properly named and placed versions of Lucy and Jonathan, she may be the most un-Mina like of all.

Penny Dreadful (2014–16)

This television series features characters, mostly adapted from nineteenth-century literature, who fight the supernatural, including Dracula. Most of the literary figures are from the later 1800s (Dr. Jekyll in 1886, Dorian Gray in 1890, and Dracula in 1897), but it also includes Dr. Frankenstein and his monster, from the novel written in 1818, a very different time. All this suggests that the creators were unconcerned with anachronisms and willing to gather up whatever they wanted from literature and folklore.

The versions of Victor Frankenstein and Dorian Gray are different takes on the characters from those found in the original source material, but they are still recognizable. Mina and Jonathan Harker, on the other hand, exist in this version, under their proper names, but their stories are wildly different. While Mina does appear in a few scenes and in extended flashbacks, with the maiden name Murray and married to Jonathan Harker, she mostly exists off-screen; Jonathan is never seen and is barely alluded to. Where the original character was an orphan, here one of the main characters is Mina's father, Sir Malcom Murray, placing her in a wealthy and titled family. Another main character is her one-time best friend, Vanessa Ives, who, instead of being rather flirty and flighty, has an intense personality, equal parts pious restraint and sexual liberation.

Both of these major characters were created for the show, with no literary antecedents, but have spun off from Mina, replacing her and Jonathan. So while it clears the low bar of giving Mina her correct name, this adaptation de-centers her from the narrative as it changes almost everything about her circumstances and personality.

The first season focuses on the group's attempt to find and rescue Mina, who has disappeared and is in under the power of a not-yet-revealed vampire master. It is explained that, after her marriage, "she became embroiled with another man . . . she has become his slave." Mina is shown with vampiric powers, but also as young and seemingly vulnerable, begging for help, which is all very far from Stoker's self-sufficient character. This aligns her with the flashbacks, where she is fairly timid and conventional compared to the bold and adventurous Vanessa. In the novel, her conventional side is a result of her social class and her practical nature, but she always thinks for herself. Here, that quality is exaggerated to make her more dependent and vulnerable, much as Lucy's flirtatious qualities are extended to Vanessa's outright betrayal of her best friend, having sex with Mina's fiancé on their wedding night.

We never learn the details of how Mina encountered Dracula, although Vanessa was his real object all along, placing her in a role the Mina character often occupies in the story. But it appears that the more conventional girl gave herself fairly easily, while the passionate fallen woman is able (mostly) to resist. Count Dracula doesn't appear at all in Mina's storyline, only appearing two seasons after her death to court Vanessa in disguise. Thus, Mina is not only decentered, but mostly erased from what had been her story.

In connection with her, since Jonathan never appears or has any effect on anything, his existence could have been left out completely. One suspects he exists only to align this story with the general outline of Stoker's novel, even though this leads to some incongruities, such as the fact that even when Mina goes missing, her husband and her father never have any contact or communication. It would make more sense in context if she had simply remained Mina Murray.

Overall, *Penny Dreadful* feels free to diverge from the source material, just as it provides a specific version of Victorian England, not bound to historical accuracy. The separation of Vanessa Ives from the character of Mina, while borrowing some of her plot function as Dracula's target and as an intelligent woman making plans for a group of men, is probably a good idea. Unlike the Minas of so many other versions, she is free to be her own woman.

Concluding Thoughts

It is peculiar that, in the most recent examples, the "Mina" character has the proper name and is married to her canonical husband, but these Minas have personalities that diverge, arguably the most dramatically, from the original text. Over time, the biographical basics of Mina Murray have been restored, but there appears to be less of an interest in Stoker's original characterization.

Apart from the vampire of the title, none of the human individuals in *Dracula* are treated with the reverence granted to some literary characters. The adapted Minas and Lucys certainly don't have the kind of character integrity, sticking closely to established textual identities, that one tends to see with Jane Eyre or Elizabeth Bennett in their various iterations. Despite containing a large cast, adaptations of *Pride and Prejudice* don't switch out Elizabeth for Jane or even swap Mary and Lydia. Sir Arthur Conan Doyle's Holmes and Watson have appeared in multiple versions in multiple time periods, but their names and basic relationship consistently remain intact (barring variations like gender-swaps, which necessitate new first names).

With *Pride and Prejudice* or the Sherlock Holmes stories, perhaps, the works are still entrenched enough, and the characters distinct enough in the popular imagination, that major changes can take place, but rearranging names and basic biographic information would be off-putting to their audiences.

Adapting classic literature will always require changes as the written works are translated to a visual medium. Additionally, many creators clearly want to reshape the material according to their own styles and interests and, in doing so, will strip the existing characters down to their basics. Jonathan usually remains the young lawyer on a trip to hell; Van Helsing endures as the elderly expert on the occult; Renfield continues to lurk in the asylum, eating insects and yelling about how the blood is the life. In this context, Lucy's essential function in the plot is to be the first victim, who dies to sound the alarm, and Mina's is as the primary victim, whom the rest of the cast is trying to save.

From this basic place in the plot, Mina can go in many directions, wherever the newly revised plot needs her to go. She can be little more than a damsel in distress, terrified of the monster, or can take a more active, even transgressive role, falling in love with the monster. Either way, what is emphasized is her perceived place in the story as Dracula's ultimate victim. Once the focus is firmly placed there, her more individual traits tend to fall away, and she is slotted into whatever existing female archetype is required by the plot.

Given that the need to make changes from the original classics is well understood, it may seem strange to be concerned about the ethics of adapting classic works, but questions do arise. There is a story by the Polish science fiction writer Stanislaw Lem called "U-Write-It," about the invention of a "literary erector set" (96) that allows readers to recombine and rewrite works of literature. With it, "you take *Crime and Punishment* in hand, or *War and Peace,* and do whatever you please with the characters" (97). "Svidrigailov can marry Raskolnikov's sister . . . Anna Karenina will betray her husband not with Vronsky, but the footman, etc." Interestingly, this story far predates the rise of fan fiction and mashup culture. Here, however, even when the entertainment value of desecrating famous novels becomes clear—for example, "to have incest practiced" in "the worthy families of Dickens" (98)—the product is a flop.

The narrator suggests that for certain "eggheads" the characters are meaningful, but not "for the public at large," for whom "they are empty sounds, names without context." Without a real love for the originals, there isn't even any transgressive thrill. He explains, "For me, the union of Svidrigailov with Natasha would be a horrendous thing, but for the public it would mean no more or less than the marriage of Mr. X. and Mrs. Y" (99).

For me, the idea the union of Bram Stoker's Mina sharing an undying love with her vampire persecutor is a horrendous thing, for much the same reason that Lem singles out Dostoevsky's Svidrigailov, an unashamedly amoral rapist whose pursuit of women is the opposite of romantic. While Dracula is not a literal rapist, in the novel he does mentally manipulate women against their will and uses their bodies without their consent, and these violations can be viewed along the same spectrum, and potentially symbolizing rape. For many makers and viewers of *Dracula* adaptations, however, it is likely that Mina and Dracula are, as Lem suggests, "names without context," whose relationship can be casually rearranged.

For Mina in particular, it could also be a factor that her primary personality traits—respectable, down-to-earth, inclined to organize and analyze—aren't particularly cinematic. Film is a visual medium, and once a beautiful woman is placed onscreen in the arms of a monster, sometimes a seductive one, it is no surprise that this visually striking image draws attention, overshadowing her other aspects and parts of her story.

Many films of all kinds, though, have featured the gathering of evidence and the putting together clues, finding ways to depict the process in visual ways. The loss of Mina's central role as *Dracula*'s detective is unfortunate; even more so, that she uses her practical skills to create the plan that is used to destroy the vampire. Whatever the intent of the filmmaker or graphic novelist or playwright or what have you, this erasure detracts from her agency and her uniqueness as a character, and it is unfortunate that her original role should be so often overlooked.

Works Cited

Belford, Barbara. *Bram Stoker: A Biography of the Author of Dracula*. Cambridge, MA: Da Capo Press, 2002.

Bram Stoker's Dracula. Directed by Francis Ford Coppola; starring Gary Oldham, Winona Ryder, Anthony Hopkins, and Keanu Reeves. American Zoetrope and Columbia Pictures, 1992.

Count Dracula. Directed by Philip Saville; starring Louis Jourdan, Frank Finlay, Susan Penhaligon, Judi Bowker, and Jack Shepherd. BBC, 1977.

Deane, Hamilton; Balderston, John L.; and Stoker, Bram. *Dracula: The Vampire Play*. Garden City, NY: Nelson Doubleday, 1977.

Dracula. Directed by Tod Browning; starring Bela Lugosi, David Manners, Helen Chandler, and Dwight Frye. Universal Pictures, 1931.

Dracula. Directed by John Badham; starring Frank Langella, Laurence Olivier, Donald Pleasence, and Kate Nelligan. The Mirisch Company and Universal Pictures, 1979.

Horror of Dracula. Directed by Terence Fisher; starring Peter Cushing, Michael Gough, Melissa Stribling, and Christopher Lee. Hammer Film Productions, 1958.

Lem, Stanislaw, and Michael Kandel. "U-Write-It." In *A Perfect Vacuum*. New York: Harvest/HBJ, 1979. 96–101.

Logan, John, creator. *Penny Dreadful*. Showtime, 2014.

Nosferatu: A Symphony of Horror. Directed by F. W. Murnau; starring Max Schreck, Gustav von Wangenheim, and Greta Schröder. Prana Film, 1922.

Stoker, Bram. *Dracula*. Oxford: Oxford University Press, 1983.

A Man Known by His Absence

Géza A. G. Reilly

TODD VICK. *Renegades and Rogues: The Life and Legacy of Robert E. Howard.* Austin: University of Texas Press, 2021. 266 pp. $29.95 hc. ISBN: 9781477321959.

Robert E. Howard's life persists in being riddled with mythology to the extent that he is a cipher even to some diehard fans of his writing. Perhaps this has been due to the fact that though there have been several biographies of his life—more than I had known about before sitting down to write this review, in fact—there has not yet been a *definitive* biography of the life of Robert E. Howard. Contrast this to Howard's contemporary and friend, H. P. Lovecraft, who was graced with several biographies of varying quality before S. T. Joshi's definitive *I Am Providence* (an expanded version of an earlier biography by Joshi) was published. Now, the facts of Lovecraft's entire life are not only accessible, but they are readily available in one two-volume opus. Not so with Robert E. Howard, and while Todd Vick's *Renegades and Rogues* is a welcome addition to the corpus of biographies of the writer, it is anything but definitive.

In fact, I ended up thinking of Vick's offering as an excellent companion volume to something like Mark Finn's *Blood and Thunder* biography. Certainly, Vick is using source documents to build his text that were presumably not available to Finn (at least when Finn wrote the first edition of his book), but that does not make *Renegades and Rogues* as robust as one would like for a one-and-done portrayal of a historical figure. Indeed, I think that it is telling that the last three chapters of Vick's book focus on events occurring after Howard's death. To be fair, the subtitle of the book is *The Life and* Legacy *of Robert E. Howard,* so it is not untoward for Vick to spend time discussing the aftermath of Howard's suicide, subjecting a selection of his stories to quasi-analysis, or investigating the fandom that has grown up around Howard's creations. Still, I think that perhaps the reader would have been better off if those pages had been spent apprehending the subject of the book more directly.

Perhaps that is unkind, especially since the circumspect quality of Vick's biography is something that I found quite compelling. Where other biographies put Howard center stage, keeping the proverbial light of investigation on the man himself, Vick describes Howard via an interrogation of the world and people around him. This inverse or photo negative method of constructing the image of a life can work quite well, and it does so here; I found Vick's biography leaving me with a *Jacob's Room*–style impression of Howard. It was as if I were seeing the man only by observing how he had been poured into the mold of life, knowing him from the outline creation had put around him.

This method of biographical investigation can indeed be insightful, and it would be a disservice to deny Vick the praise he deserves on this level. A significant amount of insight is presented on how Howard developed into the man and writer that he was, and a wonderful amount of time is spent on the inspiration people and places gave him for some of his most famous works. Equally, the personalities he became acquainted with and the landscapes he lived in help define and explain the views and opinions he would eventually express. If *Renegades and Rogues* can be said to be a photo negative presentation of the life of Robert E. Howard, then Vick is to be commended for the clarity of and detail within that image.

This is not to say that everything is included within that photo negative, however. I was disappointed to see how little space was given to discussing some of Howard's genuine interests in life, such as boxing and athletics in general. Equally, I was struck by how next to no discussion is given to some of Howard's streams of fictional output, such as his sailor stories, his El Borak stories, and even his westerns. Granted, Vick does dive deep into the creation of Howard's most popular creations, such as Conan (of course), Kull, and Bran Mak Morn (to be expected), and even some of his lesser-known weird stories. Still, I was left thinking that more could have been said along specific directions.

That is, ultimately, why I became convinced that *Renegades and Rogues* is an excellent companion biography. It is outstanding at what it does, but its efforts are not quite enough to give a full understanding of its subject. At its best, *Renegades and Rogues* leaves the reader in a place similar to where one ends up at the end of the aforementioned Virginia Woolf novel: awash in the certainty that there must have been *more* to the subject of the text than has been shown and mired in the tragedy that it is too late to know him directly. There is much to be said in this slim biography, but it is not quite enough to stand on its own.

Perhaps it would be safe to say that Robert E. Howard, for all his interesting qualities, was not quite larger-than-life as his creations were. Certainly, the man has seemed to fade into the background while his stories and characters, in replication, imitation, and bastardization, have taken up ever more cultural capital over the decades since his death. Still, much of interest can be said about Howard, the people who drove him, and the world that shaped him. There was and is a fascinating heart and mind at work behind the words, and that heart and mind should be known by those who are arrested by the tales left behind. Interested readers could do much, much worse than start learning about the outsider of Cross Plains who struggled valiantly to be a Texan writer of the first rank via *Renegades and Rogues*. Vick's biography even has a place on the shelves of the most knowledgeable of Howard devotees. It is just that, at the end of the day, it is far from being enough of a last word.

Sure It's Dark, But Is It Horror?

Tony Fonseca

SEAN PADRAIC BIRNE. *I Would Haunt You If I Could*. Pickering, ON: Undertow Publications, 2021. 254 pp. $17.95 tpb. ISBN: 9781988964263.

Sean Padraic Birne's short story collection *I Would Haunt You If I Could* is appropriately titled, as readers will be hard pressed to view the collection as belonging to the horror genre. While they are well written, for Birne is a master wordsmith, and while some of them contain supernatural elements, only a couple of the stories are in any way haunting, scary, or disquieting. Rather, most read like toned down versions of Rod Serling's *Twilight Zone* tales, sometimes combined with touches of Edgar Allan Poe's psychological narratives, minus the horror. In fact, the main impression I get from each of the stories is that getting trapped in your own head tends toward fostering a dark place within, one that can border on horror—if combined with horrifying realizations or details and a sense of impending doom. The late dark fantasist (think magical realism with a tinge of horror or terror) Robert Aickman was the master of this, and in fact it was tempting to view Birne's stories through this lens; however, doing so made it clear why Aickman was a master: it's just not that easy to create truly haunting tales of magical realism. So the bottom line on *I Would Haunt You If I Could* is that it is a collection of beautifully written psychological narratives (and a few experimental short pieces; more on that later), but readers looking for horror, as the genre is usually understood, will not find it here.

A case in point is the collection's opening tale, "New to It All." It is a study in sadomasochistic psychosexual horror featuring a woman who has a predilection (and talent) for painlessly chewing off body parts and then reattaching them. Though the story, like everything else in this collection, is well written, I was left with a sense of the narrative's pointlessness.

While the idea of having body parts chewed off and then reattached by your lover is interesting fodder for a story, I was never sure why the narrator became fascinated with this particular fetish, nor was I sure whether the story's supernatural elements were a clear metaphor for the narrator's state of mind (there is a hint, as the male narrator does have a tendency to fall apart briefly after failed relationships, but it is left too subtle, since the story ends before the threat of his falling apart literally occurs). In addition, no clear reason is ever given as to why the relationship ends. We are told enough to know there are trust issues, but given the narrator's past, those trust issues don't logically follow; the breakup just seems to happen because it is needed to move the plot forward.

"Like a Zip" has similar weaknesses. While it also has a clear supernatural element that is horrifying in its repulsiveness (a woman discovers that she can simply peel off her skin), it also seems to have no purpose other than that of repulsive imagery. Despite its title, it has no controlling metaphor because there is nothing to suggest why this particular character would discover this ability, and more importantly, why she would then decide to pursue it; she simply decides that she is going to peel off her skin. As in "New to It All," the narrative comes across as something weird that happened, with little to no significance other than to the tale's main character. This type of issue occurs again in "Holes," where again a physical deformity is introduced, without any sense of what it means because of a lack of a metaphorical significance. This results in a story about a couple who develop spots on their bodies that eventually turn into holes—just something that happened, nothing more.

"The Turn" is probably the most representative story in the collection in that it is all about atmosphere and an interior dialogue of a dark nature and there isn't really any threat or supernatural element (and, in fact, anyone would be hard pressed to call this horror or even dark fantasy). It is simply a well-written story about a woman who has an argument with her partner, drinks too much, and then goes for a midnight drive where she runs out of gas and then must figure out what to do. While there is a very subtle hint of a possible ghostly presence, if a ghost were what was intended here, the story misses the mark.

The collection's only true study in horror (as in haunting, disquieting, repulsive, and scary) is its final piece, "Other Houses." Here Birne creates a world where grieving has somehow led the narrator's father to create alternate worlds where important events, including family deaths, never happened (I say "somehow" because the process is never explained—it just made possible because of the weird architecture of the father's house, an architecture that leads to secret stairwells and hidden rooms). After the father's death, the narrator, while going through the estate, discovers a camera that was used to take photos of an alternate reality and eventually stumbles on the secret stairwell. After a confrontation with her sister, who knew of the father's practices, she comes to understand the tenuousness of reality. The story ends with the most horrifying image in the collection—a meeting with her mother, who was the father's first attempt at "reanimation" through alternative reality. Unfortunately, as the sister points out, it wasn't a completely successful attempt.

This is not to say that fans of dark psychological literature won't find a good bit to enjoy in this collection, for it does contain some gems, such as the aforementioned "The Turn." The collection's best story is its second one, "Out of the Blue," which can best be described as dark magical realism. It deals very honestly and powerfully with death, grieving, and memory, as the narrator's father returns from the dead—in a very unremarkable fashion. The father is just a physical presence, a directionless zombie who must be led from room to room, otherwise he just sits or stands wherever he happens to be and stares off blankly. The narrator keeps him in the attic until necessity dictates that he must be moved to the cellar. Here, there is some strong symbolism because it turns out that the attic is the only cluttered room in a tidy house (the house belonged to the narrator's father, a neat, organized man). Unfortunately, the idea of a cluttered mind existing in an organized body is never clearly tied to the father's living state. This is a bit of a disappointment, because that tie-in would have made this story a masterpiece, something reminiscent of the works of Gary A. Braunbeck at his best. The other disappointment in the story is that the reason why the father returns is never even entertained. His reappearance is just something that happened. That said, the final image of the narrator taking his daughter into the cellar to meet her grandfather is both disturbing and beautiful.

"Hand-Me-Down" could have easily been the second-best story in the collection, but it falls flat because nothing ever really happens—it's all build-up. A cursed object story, it does have a haunting quality to it, but the haunting is never explained. However, as an interior dialogue piece with a dark theme, it reads like a Poe story. The only problem is that it lacks the impact of a surprise ending that would bring the horror home. Likewise, "I Would Haunt You If I Could" is a good story, but it is only tangentially related to horror. However, it does showcase the author's ability to write from both the male and female perspective, as even a careful reader would have no idea what the sex of the protagonist is until about one-third of the way through. Basically, Birne here uses the trope of telekinesis as a method of exploring a character who may or may not be supernaturally gifted (she may only be insane due to a long-standing dysfunctional relationship with a controlling mother). Unfortunately, the story is so much an interior dialogue that the reality of the telekinesis is not clear. After finishing the story, I was unable to tell whether the narrator had any powers or is simply unreliable—a person who imagines she has a powerful method to deal with her frustration and anger.

As it turns out, the collection's second-best tale is not a horror story at all, but rather a study in terror and psychological stalking. "Dollface" uses the trope of the cursed doll that cannot be destroyed but turns it on its head. Instead of a cursed doll, here Birne cleverly has a female character play with the mind of the narrator's male neighbor and friend, an unhappily married man (who wants to keep his family nonetheless) who has had an affair with his sister-in-law and has gotten her pregnant. The two have apparently had a tiff of some sort, as she is angry enough to inform him of her pregnancy by gifting his daughter a special doll. This causes him to lose his mind, believing the doll to be an evil presence that is impossible to kill. What makes this story effective is that here, instead of having the narrative be an internal monologue, like the rest of the stories, it is told from the point of view of an outsider—someone who, like the reader, is forced to waver between a realistic and a supernatural explanation for the doll.

For fans of experimental fiction, *à la* Donald Barthelme's *Sixty Stories,* Birne's collection offers "Company," "I Told You Not to Go," and "Lucida." These short prose experiments stand in contrast to the rest of the collection, and unfortunately fans of story and character development will probably find them a disappointment. Overall, I enjoyed *I Would Haunt You If I Could* for its writing style (very few books have as many beautifully written passages) and its dark psychology. However, I would warn fans of horror that they will not get what they came for if they pick it up hoping to read a good collection of horror stories. That said, if readers pick it up thinking they will read some expertly written, highly engaging, dark stories with a slightly menacing quality, they won't be disappointed.

About the Contributors

Ramsey Campbell is an English horror fiction writer, editor, and critic who has been writing for well over fifty years. He is frequently cited as one of the leading writers in the field. His website is www.ramseycampbell.com.

Peter Cannon is a senior editor at *Publishers Weekly,* where he assigns and edits the reviews in the Mystery/Thriller category. He is also the author of *H. P. Lovecraft,* a critical study in Twayne's United States Authors Series, and other works related to Lovecraft.

Philip Challinor has published several articles on the work of Robert Aickman, some of which were collected in the chapbook *Akin to Poetry* (2010). He posts satire, fiction, and assorted grumbles on a blog, The Curmudgeon, and his longer fiction is available at Lulu.com.

Tony Fonseca has co-authored three volumes of *Hooked on Horror* (with June Pulliam), as well as *Read On . . . Horror,* and has contributed to *Icons of Horror and the Supernatural* and *Encyclopedia of the Vampire*. His study of Richard Matheson (with June Pulliam) has appeared from Rowman & Littlefield.

Edward Guimont recently received his Ph.D. from the University of Connecticut Department of History.

Karen Joan Kohoutek, an independent scholar and poet, has published about weird fiction in various journals and literary websites. Recent and upcoming publications have been on subjects including the Gamera films, the Robert E. Howard/H. P. Lovecraft correspondence, folk magic in the novels of Ishmael Reed, and the proto-Gothic writer Charles Brockden Brown. She lives in Fargo, North Dakota.

Javier Martinez was managing editor of *Extrapolation* for fifteen years. A former department chair, college dean, and university provost, he is currently Professor of English in the

Department of Literatures & Cultural Studies at the University of Texas Rio Grande Valley.

Michael D. Miller is an adjunct professor and NEH medievalist summer scholar with numerous one-act play productions, awards, including several optioned screenplays to his credit, and he has written the *Realms of Fantasy RPG* for Mythopoeia Games Publications. His poetry has appeared *Spectral Realms* and scholarly publications in the *Lovecraft Annual*.

Jon Padgett is the Editor-in-Chief of Grimscribe Press, which publishes *Vastarien: A Literary Journal,* a source of critical study and creative response to the work of Thomas Ligotti. Padgett's first short story collection, *The Secret of Ventriloquism,* was named the Best Fiction Book of the Year by *Rue Morgue Magazine.*

Daniel Pietersen is a writer of weird fiction and horror philosophy. He has a blog of fragmentary work and other thoughts at constantuniversity.wordpress.com.

June Pulliam teaches courses on horror fiction at Louisiana State University. She is the author of *Monstrous Bodies: Feminine Power in Young Adult Horror Fiction,* as well as many articles on fantastic young adult fiction, Roald Dahl, and zombie studies.

Géza A. G. Reilly is a writer and critic with an interest in twentieth-century American genre literature. A Canadian expatriate, he now lives in the wilds of Florida with his wife, Andrea, and their cat, Mim.

Darrell Schweitzer is an American writer, editor, and critic in the field of speculative fiction. Much of his focus has been on dark fantasy and horror, although he does also work in science fiction and fantasy.

Joe Shea (The joey Zone) is an artist and illustrator. Samples of his work can be found at www.joeyzoneillustration.com.

Oliver Sheppard is a poet based in Texas. He is the author of the Elgin Award nominated *Thirteen Nocturnes* and writes for *Post-Punk(dot)com, CVLT Nation,* and others.

www.ingramcontent.com/pod-product-compliance
Lightning Source LLC
LaVergne TN
LVHW020650100826
845148LV00012B/2413